OZYMANDIAS

THOMAS F. MONTELEONE

DOUBLEDAY & COMPANY, INC.

GARDEN CITY, NEW YORK

1981

All of the characters in this book
are fictitious, and any resemblance
to actual persons, living or dead,
is purely coincidental.

Library of Congress Cataloging in Publication Data
Monteleone, Thomas F.
    Ozymandias.
        I. Title.
PS3563.O542O97   813'.54
AACR2
ISBN: 0-385-15768-1
Library of Congress Catalog Card Number 80–1658

First Edition

OZYMANDIAS

*This is for
Roy Torgeson,
Editor, Agent,
And all-around Crazy Person*

I met a traveller from an antique land
Who said: Two vast and trunkless legs of stone
Stand in the desert . . . Near them, on the sand,
Half-sunk, a shattered visage lies, whose frown,
And wrinkled lip, and sneer of cold command,
Tell that its sculptor well those passions read
Which yet survive, stamped on these lifeless things,
The hand that mocked them, and the heart that fed:
And on the pedestal these words appear:
"My name is Ozymandias, king of kings:
Look on my works, ye Mighty, and despair!"
Nothing beside remains. Round the decay
Of that colossal wreck, boundless and bare
The lone and level sands stretch far away.

—Percy Bysshe Shelley
First age poet

There seems to be a great danger in digging up the past. It is an unsettling feeling to sift through the bones of other men, for it is often like a mirror in which one sees his own reflected future. Great was the power of those who walked before us. Even now, as some of us walk among their empty-husked cities, the skeletons of their machines, we can clearly see the final destiny, the entropic corruption that awaits all things. It seems that we cannot learn from the lessons called history, and that is why we must leave them buried.

—excerpt from The Warning
by Prathes of Borat

OZYMANDIAS

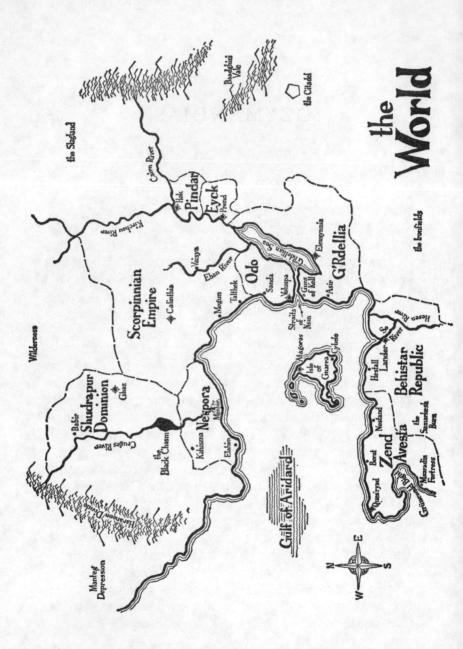

the
World

the Shagland

Baadghazi
Vale

the Citadel

Caim River

Pindar

Hok

Eyck

Prend

K'rchou River

Scorpinnian
Empire

Vaisya

Calinthia

Eban River

Odo

Grdellian Sea

Eleusynnia

Sanda

Asir

G'Rdellia

Mogtan

Talthek

Voluspa

Guns of Kell

the frontfields

Straits
of
Nsin

Hezen River

Wilderness

Alagoras

Isle
of
Gnarra

Cybele

Hesfall

Landor

Shudrapur
Dominion

Babir

Ghaz

Nostand

Behistar
Republic

Cruljes River

Kahisma

Nespora

Mt.
Menaim

Zend

Borat

Avesta

the
Samarkesh
Barra

the
Black Chasm

Elahim

Nazir
Fortress

Beor
River

Quan'ryad

Gruesalem Divide

Gulf of Aridard

Grunwalin

Manteg
Depression

N

W   E

S

PROLOGUE

It is often said that global conflicts can be traced back to small, seemingly insignificant events. These singular, usually unrelated incidents slowly coalesce into something larger than the sum of its parts, which in turn becomes a major catalytic force—a precursor to a great war.

Perhaps it is too early to ascertain, but I suspect that the news of the Stoor Expedition, and its subsequent impact on the World, will be one of these seemingly insignificant events which will lead us all into another conflagration. For many years after the fact, the details of the Stoor Expedition were tangled in a web of rumor and the ubiquitous tavern tale. There were, consequently, few among the learned and scholarly-minded who looked seriously into the accounts of the expedition. But fortunately, the sense of oral tradition is strong in the World, and reports continued to filter upward, into the domains of the historians, academicians, and scholars, which told of a quest of four soldiers of fortune to discover the last functioning remnant of the First Age—a place called the Citadel.

The Citadel was reported to have been a vast fortress, filled with the magical devices and machines of the First Age and administered by a complex entity known only as Guardian. The leader of the quest was none other than the famed explorer and raconteur Stoor of Hadaan, who had made a handsome living for more than a generation under the employ of various monarchs and men of wealth throughout the civilized World. Under various imprimaturs, Stoor had sought out artifacts of the First Age, which he brought back to his employers for whatever use they wished. Some of the more frivolous men used the First Age objects as little more than trinkets—doorstops, hatracks, conversation pieces—regarded as quaint antiques, but nothing more. Other, more inspired employers handed over Stoor's discoveries to their tinkerers and scientists, from which modern adaptations of First Age ingenuity have been allowed to brighten our lives.

The wealthy agricultural barons and dukes of Shudrapur Dominion were among the most trifling, and it is difficult to say what First Age marvels are languishing behind their palace doors, or are supporting the burnooses of ignorant, carefree sheikhs. The World should therefore be thankful for the more forward-looking nations such as Zend Avesta and Odo for implementing Stoor's discoveries in a more useful fashion. In some parts of the World, the people are enjoying the labors of electricity, combustion engines, and sun-powered generators. Our more optimistic philosophers predict that within the next century the entire known World will be well upon the path first trod by our mighty ancestors.

But I digress. The tale at hand concerns the most recent feats of Stoor and his small expedition. It was some years after the completion of the journey that the first conclusive evidence of the expedition came to light. The record shows that one member of the original quest for the Citadel was a merchant seaman by the name of Varian Hamer, a man whose name appears on many a ship's manifest which has plied the Gulf of Aridard. After the wreck of the *Yellow Swan,* off the coast of Nespora, debris from the ill-fated ship littered the beaches for the better part of a week. One of the most important pieces of salvage was a sailor's trunk, sealed tightly against the seawater, which was discovered by a merchant from Mentor out on a beachcombing vacation. The contents of the trunk contained the usual mundane possessions of a seaman and one curious thing: a notebook filled with the writings of Várian Hamer.

The merchant, after having read the entire notebook, was intelligent enough to recognize the value of his fortunate discovery, and brought it immediately to a friend who worked as a historian at the City University in Mentor. The Notebooks, kept in a diary form, construct a precise log of the Stoor Expedition, from the point at which Hamer met the famed Stoor in a tavern in Ques'ryad. There were meticulous notations, giving time and place and detailing every important incident during the expedition. There was a short period of confusion after the discovery of the Hamer Notebooks, during which some scholars and historians claimed that the logs were nothing more than an elaborate hoax. Indeed, these doubters were not stilled until the great Stoor himself came forth and verified the accounts of the Hamer Notebooks.

But I digress once again.

Varian Hamer reported meeting a strange, cowled figure who called himself Kartaphilos, and who further claimed to have been in the service of the First Age masters. Kartaphilos, so he said, had been wandering the World in search of men who could come to the aid of Guardian for untold centuries. My scribes and researchers at the Great Library in Voluspa report that the name Kartaphilos is an ancient First Age term often interchanged with the name Ahaseurus, who was in turn also known as the Wandering Jew. Efforts to reveal the meaning of the word "jew" have been thus far unsuccessful, although the scholar might rightly intuit that a "jew" is some kind of First Age robot or cyborg—in light of what is now known of Kartaphilos.

At any rate, say the Notebooks, Kartaphilos left Hamer with vague references as to the location of the Citadel before disappearing into the crowds of the teeming docks at

Mentor. Although Hamer had been given a demonstration
of Kartaphilos' cyborg nature, the seaman did not act
directly on the information thereby imparted. It was not
until he met Stoor of Hadaan in the port-city tavern that
the notion of a real expedition to the Citadel became a reality.

It is true that the quest would not have been possible
without the extensive knowledge and list of contacts open
to old Stoor. The man had influence with most of the powerful, wealthy rulers and financiers of the age, and when
one has influence, it is understood that one might owe
favors and, conversely, have favors owed.

Stoor had enough favors owed to have his expedition
financed and outfitted with capable gear, including several
recycled First Age artifacts. They struck out east from
Zend Avesta, leaving the friendly confines of civilization
for the beastly furnace of the Samarkesh Burn, the most
hostile desert in the known World, and a place from which
few explorers emerge. But the Burn was an old opponent
to Stoor and he navigated his small party of four through it
with little difficulty. From that point, they continued east
through the lower realms of the Behistar Republic, which
at that time was still rigidly held in check by the Interdict
—a Worldwide sanction against any bellicose activity outside the borders of the ironically named Republic. For the
first time in recent history, the fierce *Lutens* of Behistar
pomped through their reigns with the bit of restraint placed
firmly amid their teeth. Interdict be damned, however, the
Stoor Expedition encountered several bands of local
Raiders, who would have enjoyed appropriating the soldiers of fortune's methane-powered vehicle and its panoply
of weapons and supplies. But if we are to believe the
Hamer Notebooks, the Behistar Raiders were vanquished
convincingly.

When the Expedition reached the easternmost borders of

the Republic, there lay before them only the sand expanses
of largely uncharted, unexplored territory which led to that
part of the World known only as the Ironfields—a vast
piece of the continent that sprawls on endlessly to form the
most grotesque monument to humankind ever devised. It is
said in legend that the Ironfields are embedded with some
kind of spiritual, or perhaps metaphysical, magnet which
draws men lemminglike to the spot, where they are
suffused with the desire and the energy to carry out their
personal vision of Armageddon.

If one is to believe eyewitnesses, millions have shared a
similar vision. The Ironfields lay littered with the rusting
corpses of war machines, fleets of planes, and the bones of
unfortunate warriors. It is the place of the final testament,
the lasting escutcheon where broken dreams and forgotten
causes mingle with the drifting sands, the desiccating heat
of centuries.

It seems appropriate, then, and more than a little bit obvious, that Stoor should begin his quest for the Citadel
within or beyond the Ironfields. Such a place of mass destruction would surely offer up some clues, and indeed it
did.

The expedition passed through the Ironfields without
dire incident and eventually located the Citadel, which
contained an immense machine which Hamer refers to as
an "AI" and makes little further attempt to describe. The
machine was called Guardian and had been empowered by
its First Age builders to maintain, supervise, and protect the
city which long ago huddled about the base of the mighty
Citadel. It is difficult to imagine a machine capable of the
exploits described by Hamer, but many of the miracles of
the First Age have always seemed beyond credibility until
they have been re-created by our own scientists and
scholars. Although there is nothing in the World which
even faintly resembles the entity known as Guardian, I feel

it is safe to assume that the machine mentioned in the Hamer Notebooks most likely did exist.

The Guardian was very much concerned with the mystery that is humankind, and for many months the expedition was confined by Guardian in an effort to unravel the mystery. Upon reflection, this is quite a heady enterprise for a machine, and it is not surprising to learn that Guardian was for the most part unsuccessful. After all, need we be reminded that this selfsame mystery has been pondered by artists and philosophers from the beginning of humankind's presence on the planet?

The expedition might still be held within Guardian's quarantine were it not for the unexpected return of Kartaphilos, who aided the group of four in their escape from the Citadel. The Notebooks of Varian Hamer detail the above-listed events in rather colorful prose, despite the fact that it is not terribly literary, and I refer interested parties to the reference librarian at Voluspa for a firsthand examination of monastic facsimiles.

Although the entire corpus of the Notebooks is intrinsically fascinating, having opened doors into vaults which will provide scholars with lifetimes of fanciful speculation, I myself find the last entry to be the most cryptic, and the most chilling. Rather than attempt to paraphrase or reconstruct the kernel of meaning contained within the final passage, it serves everyone for me to simply quote that able seaman Varian Hamer:

Kartaphilos suggested the long-dormant "nucleotide vats" and the "eugenic bioneering systems" as the logical starting place for the project, and Guardian seemed to concur. When the work began, I departed the place with Tessa, Stoor, and the silent Raim, beginning a long journey back to Zend Avesta, where a different kind of army is now being assembled—an

*army of thinkers and tinkerers, of philosophers and
men of science, who will soon descend upon the treasure chest of knowledge which is the Citadel.*

*When we left the place, a half-man and a machine
were laboring to achieve the unthinkable. When we
return, I have no idea what we will find.*

I am not even sure I wish to think about it.

Regardless of what might be implied by such melodrama, it is necessary to note that Hamer's final passage
contains several presumptuous statements concerning the
fate of the Citadel. The army of scientists and thinkers
was, sadly, never assembled. It is supposition, but from the
later testimonies of Stoor, the current theory lives that the
expedition decided, along the journey homeward, to keep
the location and nature of the Citadel a secret. To the best
sources of knowledge, no further expeditions have been
launched to find the Citadel, and even though each spring
brings with it rumors of such projects, there is no evidence
to support that anyone has ever set forth, much less redis-
covered, the lair of Guardian.

Under oath and inquisition, Stoor of Hadaan steadfastly
refused to reveal the location of the Citadel, suggesting
that anyone interested in such things begin a systematic
search of the Ironfields. And so the learned world stands
upon the horn of a dilemma, having been blessed with
some knowledge on the subject and cursed with not
enough. As time passes, I suspect that even the existence of
Stoor, the expedition, and of course Guardian will fall into
that vague repository of half-truth known as Legend.

And yet, there is the nagging thought—call it the intui-
tive sixth sense of a true historian if you will—which tells
me that this singular event, this diverting sidetrack along
the wastelands of current events, will in time become one
of the catalysts which wreak mighty change upon the

World. Even now, the balances of economic power are shifting throughout the World. The nomads of the Manteg Depression speak of strange happenings in their land. The potentates of the Shudrapur Dominion are taking an interest in global Agribiz. The leaders of the Behistar are flexing warrior muscles, and making ugly noises about the Interdict.

It is truly a time of unrest.

—Excerpt from *The Tides*
by Granth of Elahim

CHAPTER 1

The Citadel at dawn: streamers of fire breaking across the jagged horizon like the beams of ancient weapons. The cool sand shifting under indifferent winds, sculpting itself about the hulks of pitted war machines and whitening bones. It is a place of desolation and silence. There is no life, no sound.

The Citadel was an immense fortress, and its five-sided bulk still rises above the desert land like a monument to the greatness that once was man's. If an errant traveler were to pass the Citadel, there would be no sign to him that the fortress still lived.

But it did live.

Inside its thick walls, deep within its honeycomb chambers, a cyborg named Kartaphilos sat at a console, plugged into a matrix of computer grids, digesting input data, analyzing results from previous experiments, and synthesizing new procedures. Kartaphilos was a regulation-specs cyborg from the First Age, whose only improvement upon basic design was the wisdom which comes with age and experience. His body was practically all synthetic materials—alloys, plastics, and silicones—except for his nervous system. Notichord, brainstem, medulla oblongata, and the brain itself were all carefully enclosed within a strong, microprocessor-monitored, self-repairing body. Covered with synthetic flesh, Kartaphilos resembled a man of perhaps fifty years, although the weathered features of his hands and face added an aspect of greater age, usually associated with sagacity. Kartaphilos had long ago taken to wearing a loosely flowing garment, much like the habits of Odonian monks, complete with hoods and thickly corded cincture. Tall and well proportioned, he was a striking figure.

"Guardian," he said softly. "I have the final data . . . The regenerative tissue experiments are positive. Viral and bacterial resistance recombinants also positive. Predictive analysis and pretest parameters indicate high probability of psychokinetic ability. The final test-series is complete."

AFFIRMATIVE, KARTAPHILOS. THANK YOU. The electronically constructed voice of the Artificial Intelligence spoke to the cyborg through a small grid on one of the consoles. WE MAY NOW BEGIN THE FINAL PHASE.

"Yes, I think we can, Guardian. I think that we can. Monitor Sector 141-D. I'll meet you there."

Kartaphilos unplugged himself from the console, stood, and slowly walked from the control room into a long corridor. He walked deliberately, knowing that there was no need to hurry, that there was ample time for all things, and that his partner in this great project was not in the least impatient.

Twenty years had passed since the Stoor Expedition had departed, and much work had been done. The plan had been to design and construct a human body for the awareness matrix of the Artificial Intelligence to occupy. Naturally the task was an ambitious one, but not impossible. The first step had been to review the access files in the population databanks, selecting somatic-psychic characteristics which were deemed most desirable. From that point, once a large sampling of priority attributes had been accumulated, Kartaphilos and Guardian cross-indexed the sampling with the tissue samples available in the cryogenic Med-Stores.

They were searching for the Ideal Male Genotype, and

although Kartaphilos knew that there was no such entity, he was certain to find a reasonable facsimile of the Ideal. The final selection was made upon assessing the genetic blueprint of a First Age squadron commander whose name had been Alterman (a rather prophetic, ironic joke, Kartaphilos immediately thought). All that remained of Commander Alterman was a frozen sliver of his pancreas, but that was more than enough to begin the task.

Kartaphilos read the basic fax-sheet:

RETRIEVAL CODE 198079
TRGF 1001887/345/876/290
ALTERMAN, PIETRAS

PHYS/00876
  2.1 meters
  104.3 kilograms
  h/brown
  e/blue
  t/mesomorphic
  hq/89.9 vg

BLOOD/OPRh
  Counts RBC
       RETIC
       PLATES
       WBC
       DIFF
  HEMATOCRIT
  HEMOGLOBIN
  INDICES MCV
       MCHC
  PROTIME
  PTT
  SED RATE

CHEMISTRY/99733

PROTEIN/64317
  ALB
  GLOB
  FIBRIN
  TOTAL
  FRAC

MISCELLANEOUS/88722
  CHOLEST
  CREAT
  GLUCOSE
  BEI
  PBI
  I
  CG

BRO

CA

CL

C

02

MG

P04

K

NΛ

C02

H20

ENZYMES/55099

  AMYLASE

  CHOLINESTERAS

  LIPASE

  PHOSPHITASE, PH ALK

  LDH

  SGOT

  SGPT

STEROIDS/78129

  ALDO

  17-OH

  17-KS

  ACTH

VITAMINS/00749

  A

  SPEC B

  C

  E

  K

  D

IBC

NPN

NJB

BILIRU, DIFF

CEPH/FLOC

THYMOL/TUR

BSP

PULMONARY/65821

TVC

TV

IC

IRV

ERV

MBC

URINE/85308

SP GR

PH

PROT

GLUC

KETONE

ELOTROLYTES

STER

ONPRG

INORG

PORYPHINS

UROBIL

5-HIAA

TRACE

The fax continued across the screen, detailing a perfect example of *Homo sapiens*. From the list would spring a living organism. To begin, Kartaphilos isolated a human ovum from an undifferentiated eggbank from cryogenic storage. Using a laser scalpel, he obliterated the nucleus of the egg. Then, obtaining a single living cell from the Alterman pancreas, Kartaphilos excised its nucleus. The pancreatic nucleus, which contained the chromosomal-genetic blueprint of Commander Alterman, was then implanted in the denucleated egg cell.

Under close monitoring by some of Guardian's lab subsystems, the fertilized ovum underwent mitotic division —dividing geometrically to form the essential blastocele. Eventually the embryonic formation would become a fetus, a perfect copy of the original Alterman. But long before this natural process was completed, Kartaphilos performed delicate genetic alterations upon the developing fetus. The genetic surgery would then ensure a variety of mental and psi abilities to create a mythical creature called *Homo superior*.

Computer-matrixed into a proton microscope, and controlling invisible laser scalpels, Kartaphilos operated upon the genes of Alterman. Delicately obliterating a piece of cytosine, or fusing several adenosines, or perhaps altering the message of a complete unit of RNA, the cyborg slowly created an anatomically perfect *Homo superior*.

The blastocele increased geometrically, passing through the limitless embryonic stages, until it assumed the configuration of the human fetus. Kartaphilos assumed the combined roles of creator, doctor, and surrogate parent as he watched the gradual development of the human body. Encased in a glass vat, floating eerily within a synthetic colloidal suspension, nurtured by an artificial placenta of sensor filaments and microcapillaries, the cloned body of Alterman grew. The time passed quickly for Kartaphilos, and for the Artificial Intelligence of Guardian, time had little meaning at all, and yet there *was* a growing impatience surging within the crystalline consciousness centers of the vast machine: it sensed its impending birth.

Once the fetus had developed to term, Kartaphilos began the application of growth-enhancement drugs—distillates from the hippocampus, esoteric enzyme recombinants, and special messenger-RNA injections which accelerated cell replication and development. Within two years of the beginning of the project, the clone of Alterman had achieved the physical stature of a twenty-two-year-old human male. The time had come to arrest the accelerative process, and this was accomplished by administering recombinant secretions from the human thymus gland—inhibitors of the aging process.

When Kartaphilos considered the project objectively, he could only marvel at the enormity, the ambition, and the obvious pride connected with the idea, i.e., the creation of a human being. In his more contemplative moments, Kartaphilos recalled the fascination of Guardian with the ancient mythologies of the First Age, of the classic tragedies and the notion of hubris as the most noble, and most telling, tragic flaw in the human spirit. The First Age poets had unswervingly pointed out the flaw of *pride* as the most ironic and inevitable cause of downfall in fortunes of humankind. Could there be a more arrogant endeavor, thought Kartaphilos? Could he be attempting anything more challenging to the gods of the human spirit? It was doubtful, and in his weaker moments he wondered what would be the outcome of the entire affair.

But they had moved too far to have second thoughts. Guardian had been preparing itself for the transformation of consciousness from AI circuitry to the watery tomb of a human brain. Final decisions were being made, being forced without thought of turning back, and Kartaphilos, having given the project its initial impetus, was now powerless to control its gathering momentum. The brain of the

Alterman clone was a *tabula rasa,* a blank slate, upon which anything could be inscribed—memories, fears, skills, knowledge, ambitions, etc. It was the artist's empty canvas, where light and life could appear as easily as it could evanesce.

But the day dawned when Kartaphilos faced the central console and spoke to Guardian.

"All is ready," he said. "Are you?"

I HAVE BEEN LONG PREPARED. I HAVE CHECKED AND RECHECKED ALL SYSTEMS. I AM PERFORMING FLAWLESSLY. SECONDARY AND TERTIARY BACKUPS ARE READY.

"So be it," said Kartaphilos. "I have done all that I can. Failure is unlikely, but I warn you of that possibility."

WE WILL NOT FAIL. WE MUST NOT FAIL.

"Very well, Guardian. I am commencing the matrix transferral . . . now."

Kartaphilos remained seated at the console, plugged into an all-systems-monitoring mode so that he might *feel* as well as read the progress of the transferral. Within the depths of the AI complex, magical changes began to take place. The databanks of the AI began disgorging the essence of their circuitry, subtly transformed into bits of electric current, which served as synaptic triggers within the blank brain of the cloned body which lay inside an egg-shaped incubating capsule. The process was slow, carried out with deliberate care—each new pulse of energy engraved upon the brain's pathways, deeper grooves, stronger patterns of response, more familiar maps of instruction and function. Layer by layer, hour by hour, the brain of the cloned body became more charged with the current of life and thought, knowledge and curiosity. The total awareness of the machine was being imprinted upon the flesh. From relay to neuron, from bit into thought, memory and fear, the transformation continued. As the cyborg, Kartaphilos, remained at his console, he could sense the *spirit* of Guardian, the ghost in the machine (as one human philosopher had phrased it) slowly ebbing away. At first the impression was that of a simple systems failure, but the sensation grew anabolically until the awareness and the functioning power of the machine became a cataract rush into the mysteries of the flesh.

Finally, the transferral ended. Kartaphilos, with the aid of his cybernetic parts, could sense an emptiness, a void, within the circuits of the AI complex. The support systems, monitoring devices, and self-maintaining functions continued, but the familiar awareness, the personalities of the machines, were oddly absent.

Guardian was gone.

Unplugging himself from the console, Kartaphilos approached the human body which was still encased in the incubation capsule. Staring through the glass walls, he could see its chest rise and fall, its fingers and toes begin to twitch.

Suddenly the body convulsed, its hands moved toward its face. Opening his eyes, the man blinked several times, then noticed Kartaphilos standing over him.

The cyborg opened the capsule and reached out his hand to the naked man.

"I see you," said the man very slowly, his bright blue eyes sparkling with the wonder and excitement of a child. He grabbed for the hand of Kartaphilos, and missed.

The cyborg nodded, smiling as he felt the surrogate pride of a parent. "Yes, I'm sure that you can . . . Here, take hold, and I'll help you out of there. Easy now . . ."

Clumsily, the man attempted to rise from the capsule. His movements were awkward and unsure. He seemed to be experimenting with the use of each new muscle. The machine awareness had a complete understanding and knowledge of human anatomy, but he was learning very quickly the difference between theory and practice.

"It . . . is . . . hard . . . ," he said with difficulty.

Kartaphilos pulled him up to a sitting position, instructed him carefully on how to come to his knees and climb from the capsule. "It will only be difficult for a short time. You are like a newborn infant in this respect. You must learn to control your new body. Speech and locomotion are the first of many abilities. But do not worry. They will come quickly."

"I . . . hope . . . so," said the man, now on his knees and staring at Kartaphilos with a look of utter dependence and trust.

"These things you will master," said the cyborg. "Later, there will be more taxing problems."

The man came to his feet, standing with a wavering, wobbly motion as the fluid in his inner ears struggled to teach his brain the meaning of equilibrium. "More . . . taxing?" he said with a look of terror. "Such . . . as?"

Kartaphilos grinned. "Such as living in the world of humans . . ."

CHAPTER 2

The words of Kartaphilos proved to be correct. As time passed, the man became adept in the mechanics of speech, of motor coordination and sensory input interpretation. He showed the child's fascination with bodily function—such as urinating and defecation—but only for a short while. Kartaphilos provided a thoughtful, systematized program of education and familiarity with the body, and the man excelled in each new phase. He proved to be extremely athletic, and only had to be shown a new ability once, thereafter mastering it with little difficulty.

One morning, during a break from the exercise program, Kartaphilos and the man sat drinking synthetic fruit juice. The cyborg had continued to call him "Guardian" more out of habit and familiarity than anything else, but on this morning, the man reacted oddly to the name.

Shaking his head, and grinning, he spoke: "My friend, Kartaphilos, I think that I'm growing uncomfortable with that name. It is a link with my . . . my past life. It's a reminder of my origins . . ."

"You will never be able to forget your origins," said Kartaphilos. "You may be able to deny them, but never forget."

"I know that. I don't mean it that way. But I've been thinking about my name, and I think I should have a new one. Something which signifies my existence and my past, and of course my future."

"That would be quite a name. I suppose that with such a

studied introduction, you no doubt have something in mind?"

"Yes, I do. How did you know?"

Kartaphilos smiled gently. In some ways, the awareness of the machine had not yet become familiar with the subtleties of human communication. "Oh, just a hunch, I suppose . . ."

"I see. Well, at any rate, I have been thinking of a name, and I wanted to discuss it with you."

"Go ahead."

"Are you familiar with the poetry of the First Age?"

Kartaphilos shook his head. "In a manner of speaking, I suppose I could say that I know *of* them. Names. Famous lines. I'm no student of the literature, if that's what you mean."

"No matter," said the man, pushing his brown hair away from his face. "There was a poet called Shelley, who wrote a short piece about the discovery of a massive relic, a colossal monument or statue of a ruler from the dawn of the First Age. There was some speculation as to who that ruler had been, although many believed it was a man called Rameses the Second . . ."

"And *that's* the name you wish to take?"

"No, not exactly. In the poem, Shelley calls the statue Ozymandias. That is the name I like."

"Well, it certainly has a lyrical ring to it. What was the connection with what you said about signifying your past and your future?"

"You should actually read the poem to see what I mean. It's odd, but in my former state of being, I could have produced it perfectly for you to read, but now I find that while I'm aware of the piece, and understand its content, I would be hard pressed to recite it for you . . ."

Kartaphilos smiled. "Yes, I know all about that sort of thing. Being human has its disadvantages—distraction and forgetfulness among them. But that's all right. You can paraphrase it if you like, and I'll catch the sense of the meaning."

The man nodded slowly as he recalled the poem. "Essentially, it tells of archeologists discovering the massive statue, and while marveling at its great size and dominance, also being aware of how time and nature have eroded it, devastated it, actually. And there is a sad, trenchant irony inscribed upon the base of the statue: *My name is Ozymandias, king of kings: Look on my works, ye Mighty, and despair!*"

Kartaphilos smiled in a small fashion, understanding. "I see . . . There *is* a wonderful analogy to be drawn, isn't there?"

The man shrugged. "*I* thought so. I'm glad that you agree."

"Very well; from now on you will be called Ozymandias."

The man smiled. "We can forget about that 'king of kings' business . . ."

Kartaphilos joined in his good humor, inwardly admiring the facility with which the machine had assumed his humanity. It was a good sign, he thought, and then amended it to be that it *seemed* like it was a good sign.

CHAPTER 3

It had been agreed that before Ozymandias would venture
out into the world of men, sufficient time would need be
taken to properly prepare for the experience. A year
passed quite eventfully as Kartaphilos trained and educated
the young man. Ozymandias assumed a beautiful control
of his body, and often reminded Kartaphilos of a sleek,
unpresupposing animal, like a mountain cat, perhaps.
When Ozymandias moved it was with the fluidlike grace
of a creature totally attuned to itself. There was a
confidence, a barely perceptible swagger, which com-
municated a sense of the superior. He was a superb athlete,
a gifted swordsman, agile and strong.

His mind had also been carefully attended to, and he
was more than simply intelligent or perceptive or knowl-
edgeable. In his long conversations and observations with
Kartaphilos, it seemed that Ozymandias's mind was a ge-
staltlike entity—that is, the sum of its power was greater
than its added parts. It was as though, in the brain of
Ozymandias, the addition of intellect, perceptivity, and
knowledge coalesced to become something far more formidable.

During the year of his training, his acclimation, he developed his personality. Kartaphilos watched him change
and evolve through a multitude of stages, always spurred
on by an insatiable curiosity of humankind. There were
times when he was very childlike and his innocence was almost a pathetic thing, and there were other moments when

his views of the World were viciously incisive, dripping with cynicism, trenchant, and coldly analytical. He was fascinated with human sexuality, and passed through a phase which must be analogous to normal adolescence, in which he seemed obsessed with his body and its functions. His knowledge of women completely nonexperiential, Ozymandias longed for the day when he would meet his first female —not out of lust or some depraved yearning, but only to satisfy his curiosity about them. He did not understand the words of Kartaphilos when the cyborg admonished him with the sentiment that there was something about the females of the species which rendered them forever inscrutable. "They are one of man's greatest, most unsolvable mysteries," said Kartaphilos as they sat at dinner one evening, and after a moment of deliberation added: "And perhaps it is best that way . . ."

Ozymandias nodded thoughtfully. "It has often been written that sexuality is one of the prime motivating factors in the history of humankind, that it is perhaps the primary lubricant upon the wheels of creativity, invention, and civilization. I have often pondered this view, and find it unacceptable."

Kartaphilos laughed lightly. "Perhaps you won't feel quite the same as time passes."

"You sound terribly patronizing."

"I intended to be."

Ozymandias sipped from his glass of wine, looking at the cyborg, acknowledging his millennia-long familiarity with humanity, but at the same time admitting the possibility that Kartaphilos had grown stagnant—such as had been said in much of the First Age literature which dealt with immortality and its attendant curses.

"When was the last time *you* saw a woman?"

"Surely you must remember," said Kartaphilos. "Her

name was Tessa, the dark-haired young one with Stoor and his friends."

"Oh yes . . . and did you take her? Sexually, I mean . . ."

Kartaphilos shook his head. "No. My mind was not on such things. Besides, I couldn't have . . ."

"Precisely. I don't think your mind has been on 'such things' in hundreds of years. And yet there is nothing wrong with your mind, Kartaphilos; it's your body, isn't it?"

"You know the answer to that," said the cyborg. "My body is not organic; it is a machine. I was not 'transformed' to be a sexual creature, Ozymandias. I was, originally, a soldier; you know that."

"And a very good soldier you were. Yes, I did know that, and I apologize. I was just being playful, I suppose. It will take some time to grow accustomed to things such as wit and cleverness. In some ways I am, as you say, nothing more than a rank adolescent."

Kartaphilos looked at him and could not tell whether or not the man was being completely serious. There was an aspect about Ozymandias which defied understanding. It was as though he were always thinking, operating in a machinelike manner, on several levels at once. When he spoke it was often with a wry, inappropriate smile, as though he were enjoying some private, macabre joke. The cyborg knew that Ozymandias had already developed some cynical notions about humankind, and he hoped that with superhuman abilities he would not fall prey to the temptations which had destroyed superior men of the past. The First Age mythologies were filled with tales of supermen who became so cynical of their surrounding humankind that they allowed their distaste to fester into overt hatred, no longer viewing their lesser fellows as unfortunate siblings in need of assistance, but rather as unnecessary vermin in need of extermination at the worst, avoidance in the least.

This was Kartaphilos's growing fear.

Ozymandias was a remarkable human, of that there was no doubt. Never before had any one man lived who possessed the range of knowledge, the millennia-stretching span of historical lessons, technological achievements, philosophical insights. Magnificent tools, thought Kartaphilos, in the hands of the right person; but in the hands of the wrong human, they could become devastating weapons. The cyborg continued to look at his creation, who placidly sipped from his wine, and Kartaphilos wondered who he himself would eventually become: Pygmalion or Dr. Frankenstein?

Kartaphilos also knew this: that eventually there must come an end to the antiseptic study of mankind, to the clinical development of becoming a person; that the time would be quickly at hand when Ozymandias would need to take leave of the theoretical and immerse himself in the experiential sea of humanity itself. There was no surrogate for that possibly traumatic plunge. Everything depended upon Ozymandias's early reaction to humankind; it was as though he were a child being touched by the Outer Hull of the World, and from those earliest encounters would his persona be thusly shaped, given substance, and directed.

"What have you been thinking?" asked Ozymandias, breaking into his companion's thoughts.

"Oh, I'm sorry . . . many things." At that moment, Kartaphilos decided that it would be wisest to simply share his fears with his young charge.

And he did.

After a lengthy explanation, in carefully couched language, Kartaphilos studied the man's features for a hint of honest reaction. The man's face remained calm and bright, but quite emotionless.

"Your fears are unfounded," he said bluntly, as though that were enough to dispel all doubt, and that the subject was beneath his need to discuss further. But then he continued, much to the relief of Kartaphilos. "And I say this not from any egocentric sphere of self-righteousness. On the contrary, I think your fears are natural ones, even the expected ones. Were I in the same position, I can assure you, I would share them. However, I possess a unique view upon this entire endeavor: my own, from the interior looking outward to all of you . . ."

Kartaphilos grasped upon the phrase *all of you,* trying to wring the true significance from its use. Interpreted wrongly, the words could make Ozymandias sound sinister indeed.

". . . and I can feel my intentions are sincere, my motivations unsullied by things such as power, avarice, or even simplistic contempt. Believe me, Kartaphilos, if you were a being such as I, it is solace enough to simply *know* that you are superior; there is no need to prove it, no need to reinforce it by taking on the stance of a wrathful god. No, my friend, in that lies madness—for all of us.

"I know why I am here, right now, at this time. As odd as it may seem, I give credence to destiny. As megalomaniacal as that may sound, I believe that there are cycles in the cosmos, in the World, and that the forces which bind us are also the forces which move us and everything within its infinite sphere. There are *times* which must eventually come of age, and there are events which must give birth to these special times. I know that *I* am one of these events— perhaps even the *principal* event, it does not matter—and that I am here in the World for a specific purpose. A destiny, if you will."

"Do you know what that purpose might be?"

Ozymandias smiled. "No, unfortunately, I do not. Not at the present. But I *will* know it. I feel that I shall know when the *time* is at hand."

"You are correct. It does sound terribly megalomaniacal." The cyborg looked away, fidgeting absently with the hem of his robes.

"I can accept that. Time will show you that you are incorrect. I perceive the World to be hanging in a critical balance point: there is poverty and wealth, power and helplessness, ignorance and knowledge, war and peace, and a hundred other antipodal elements, all stalking the World at this time. It is a precarious, fragile, and yet dangerous entity, waiting for the correct catalyst to set the balance in one direction or the other. It could be a fearful thing or a joyous one, depending upon the catalyst and its effects. *I* am the catalyst—or at least one of the major elements of it."

"I see," said Kartaphilos. "And do you have any personal preferences as to which direction the balance shall tip? Or will you be content in simply being the prime mover, the backbreaking straw of destiny?"

Ozymandias smiled. "Of course I have a preference—and for want of a better term, I should say that I am definitely in allegiance with the forces of Good, that my intentions are beneficent, and that my wish is for the triumph of the species' potentialities. It is, after all, the race of beings who created me, who gave me life and awareness. It is a debt which must be repaid."

Kartaphilos nodded. "And after the debt is repaid? What then?"

Ozymandias thought for a moment, then a sparkle flashed in his bright blue eyes. "I shall probably be misunderstood, whereupon they shall burn me at the stake." At this he threw back his head and laughed.

Kartaphilos did not join him.

"I think," he said, "that it is time for us to go out into the World."

CHAPTER 4

Their journey began soon after dawn. Riding within the bubble cab of their landcrawler, a battered relic from the Battle of Haagendaz, Kartaphilos and Ozymandias departed the Citadel, entering into the metal wilderness of the Ironfields. Ozymandias did not look back toward the ancient fortress, the edifice which until recently had been his body and his prison. It was as though he were a creature in metamorphosis; like an insect departing its amber husk, its cocoon of an earlier stage of life, he regarded the Citadel with total indifference.

Kartaphilos looked back many times, until the sand-colored walls were lost in the convection currents of the horizon. The cyborg wanted to engrave the site upon his mind, to preserve it like a photograph, because he could not escape the feeling that he would never see it again.

Ozymandias, on the other hand, shared no such premonitions or ominous feelings; at least he did not outwardly display them. In the early stages of their journey, the newly created man almost glowed with enthusiasm and a sense of *wonder* about the World, even though their battered landcrawler had not yet carried them away from the stark desolation of the Ironfields. There was a youthful innocence about Ozymandias during these early days that was almost oxymoronic in quality. Although he seemed to be profoundly affected by the stark diorama of death, by the endless gravemarkers of broken, twisted machines, of shattered bones, he was also like a child gazing through a shopwindow, full of unimagined joy and flushed with pure *experience* of the moment. There were instances, of course, when he gazed upon the half-buried remnants of the old Armageddons and recalled Shelley's poem, remembered the cold imagery of which his name had come, and was moved to somber reflection; it was as if he were reaffirming his own self-conceived mission in the world.

Look on my works, ye Mighty, and despair!

To their left, trapped in a sweeping dune of sand, the twisted hull of a great black aircraft baking in the oven heat of midday. Ozymandias stared at the massive ship, its command-deck blisters bulging like hyperthyroid eyes, its nose like a shattered pterodactyl's beak. There was an eerie animism about the wreck, and it seemed to look at Ozymandias with the baleful eyes 'of a creature abandoned by its masters and left to die alone, and never understanding why.

Presently, they passed the blackened turret of a half-buried war machine, its hatch thrown open to reveal the figure of a fire-fused skeleton, its right arm still outstretched in a desperate reach for safety. To Ozymandias, traveling through the Ironfields was like visiting the gallery of some singularly macabre sculptor—an artist whose joy had been to depict the last moments of men and their machines, to capture that final instant in which perfection became chaos, in which light became darkness, breath became an eternity of silence. Interestingly, the Ironfields were constantly shifting, changing, under the subtle grain-by-grain movements of the sand. Over the centuries, new wrecks would be slowly, artfully uncovered while old exhibits would be consumed by growing dunes. It was said in the legends of men that countless armies had met and fought here, that the great, sandy plain had drawn warriors to its soil as a magnet attracts iron filings and carefully arrays them into classic patterns.

Ozymandias considered the never-ending, always-changing gallery of final moments, trying to imagine the patterns of clashing armies. The Ironfields. How many times had it been filled with the crazy-quilt phalanxes of men, their division colors checkering the field, lances and antennae piercing the dead air? Ozymandias could almost hear the clank of steel and the anguished cries of men.

Ozymandias knew that he was one of the few men to have ever looked upon the ruin of the Ironfields, one of the few men to know that the massive graveyard actually existed. The location and the age of the place had long ago been lost to the historians of the World, but its grim presence persisted in legend and fable. It had been said through the centuries that any man who walked among the ancient wrecks would never consider war again.

Ozymandias asked Kartaphilos: "You saw the last battle here, didn't you?"

"Part of it . . . before you dispatched me for reinforcements."

"What was it like?"

Kartaphilos gestured in front of the windshield. "You can *see* what it was like."

"How many times have they fought here?"

Kartaphilos shook his head. "No one knows for certain. If you were to excavate this area, I'm sure you would find level after level of metal and bones, laid in like geologic strata."

"Even though we know the reasons, one is tempted to ask why," said Ozymandias. "Are differences so great among humans that they must resort to war so many times?"

"Of course. Look at the World of today: a groveling pit of ragtag nations, all huddled about the Aridard Gulf like beggars. They have no idea what lies beyond the fringes of their borders. It is a big planet, but most of it has lain unexplored for the last one thousand years."

"One would think that after all this time, there might have evolved some kind of political system, perhaps even an economic plan which would survive, and possibly become viable."

Kartaphilos laughed. "I fear you have not been a man long enough to understand the subtleties involved. It has been said by many philosophers—nihilists, by nature, I would assume—that there will never be a workable, agreeable political system as long as it is being administered by humans."

"Sounds cynical enough for one who's been around as long as you . . ."

Kartaphilos smiled. "You are as young as I am old, my friend, but I think you will come to the same conclusion in very short order."

"Why do you say that?"

"Because the World we are going to see is a vile place. It is a tattered remnant of what they call the First Age, the era of expansive technology of which we both owe our very existence. Except in a few of the more enlightened countries, the masses are ignorant, poorly fed, and semiliterate at best. There are distinct lines of class and breeding which date back to the feudal hierarchies of the First Dark Ages. Greed and power are the principal motivators among the upper classes, and beneficence is almost a forgotten term in their lexicons. Superstition and magic make strange bedfellows with science, but that is the state of the art in the current World. Men will believe in wizardry as quickly as they would a dry-cell battery. To most of them, there is no difference between the two."

"It all derives from the lack of concerted effort," said Ozymandias. "When the World was rebuilding from the last time of wars, there was too much fragmentation. Too much was lost, isolated, or just ignored. Hence, the various subsystems of civilization have been advanced at different rather than concurrent rates."

"You sound so professorial . . . please, don't talk like that when we are around other humans. They'll pin you for an odd one very quickly."

Ozymandias grinned and felt himself blush slightly. "I'm sorry. It's just that I have such good recall, probably a carry-over from my cybernetic days, that I tend to phrase ideas in the same language as the databanks."

"It's something you will probably get over, the more you converse in the less formal languages of humankind."

"I have been wondering about that," said Ozymandias.

"About what?"

"About how I will react to the World, and how it will react to me."

"They will not know who you really are. They would not understand, anyway."

"That's obvious, but what shall we tell the people we en-counter? Who are we, and from where have we come?"

"That is not much of a problem," said Kartaphilos. "Take it from one who has wandered throughout the known World. It is a World such as this one which breeds a separate race of nomads and drifters. The cities are filled with foreigners, and the docks and marketplaces are alive with many dialects. As long as we remain in the larger cities, no one will seriously question our presence."

"Yes, but shouldn't we have a trade, a cover of some sort?"

"It may prove to be necessary at some point. Do you have any ideas?"

Ozymandias smiled. "We could be mercenaries, couldn't we? Metalsmiths? Traders?"

"We have no wares. No weapons or tools that would

identify us as such." Kartaphilos shook his head. "No, I think we should keep things vague. Just say that we are 'travelers' and that we are out looking at the World—which is basically true."

"But suppose someone asks us where we came from—originally, I mean?"

Kartaphilos shrugged. "Pick a place. It does not matter —as long as it is far away from wherever we are at the moment. If we get caught in our lie, we can always flee. It is a big enough World."

Ozymandias laughed. "I hope it proves to be just that."

They rode in silence for a while, until the Ironfields began to thin out and the fragments of war became less obvious. They were angling toward the north, and would eventually reach the G'Rdellian Sea, and the borders of its namesake. The first city within reach of them was Eleusynnia, and it was there that Kartaphilos planned to initiate his charge.

That evening, after camp had been made and Ozymandias had eaten from the ration paks, they settled down for sleep. Sleep was the one aspect of humanity which Ozymandias had never fully accepted. He railed against the idea that roughly one third of one's life was spent doing *nothing,* and he had once told Kartaphilos that if possible he would use his talents and his facilities to search for a "cure" for sleep, so that he might never suffer from it again. Kartaphilos did not share his feelings on the matter, and in fact, welcomed the brief periods in which his microfusion reactors entered stasis, allowing the systems to recharge and regenerate any lost tissue circuitry. Being an immortal for all practical purposes, Kartaphilos did not eschew brief respites from the constant onslaught of experience called consciousness.

And so, as they settled in for the evening, under the flanking moonshadows of their landcrawler, Kartaphilos suggested that each of them should get into the habit of keeping a watch.

"But why?" asked Ozymandias. "We are as isolated as we shall ever be."

"Not really. There are nomad bands of marauders. They have no nation, no home, and they are true pirates, living off the misfortune of others. A misfortune which they are only most happy to create. There are also the isolated predators—mutated beasts, flying things that only hunt in the cool of the desert nights. No, my friend, I think it's wise that we begin to keep a watch.

"If for no other reason, it will be good training, for the closer we move to civilization, the more opportunity will there be for us to be overtaken by some outside force."

"That sounds overly paranoid to me."

Kartaphilos stared at his companion, unsmiling. "Believe me. I have lived a long time. I have not achieved this lofty age by being careless. Call it paranoia if you wish. I call it survival instinct."

Ozymandias considered the words and knew that his friend was correct. Ozymandias was still a child of the human World. All the millennia of accumulated, nonexperiential knowledge was not worth a damn in terms of *instinct*. That was something one acquired simply by living.

The night passed without incident—as did the next twelve. They were now within the borders of G'Rdellia, and would soon be reaching the outskirts of the jewel upon the sea—Eleusynnia, the City of Light.

Evening fell upon the rolling plains that flowed down to the fertile shores of the sea, and the two travelers made their camp. For the past several days, they were seeing more and more game, more fauna and vegetation. The earth seemed to be coming to life in this part of the World, having long ago licked its wounds and banished the memories of the old wars. The sky was often flecked with leathery-winged *tomars*, scavenging quasi-reptiles which fed on the carrion of other predators. There were also the tracks and remnants of prairie wolves, the nightly howls of *cragars*, and other hungry creatures born of past nightmares.

Kartaphilos sat rigidly in the cab of the 'crawler, trancelike as his fuel cells recharged, his body performing the small self-repairs which maintained his man-machine existence.

And so Ozymandias kept the watch, a small sniper's rifle cradled in his arms, his bright blue eyes scanning the dark horizon as he listened to the sounds of the night. Moonlight fell upon the slope of the plain and was lost in the tangles of brush, in the limbs of the occasional tree. He looked to his left and thought he detected movement from beyond the silhouetted sculpture of a briarwood. There was no wind and the trees had no sway: nothing should be moving, and suddenly Ozymandias grew tense, concentrating on the small point of darkness which now seemed to be bobbing easily along a faraway ridge. The object paused and descended down a slope, entering the bottom of the small valley which led up the encampment on the plain.

Whatever kind of creature it was, Ozymandias knew, it had sensed their position and had decided to investigate, out of either curiosity or hunger.

"Kartaphilos!"

There was no answer from the cab.

Ozymandias stood, feeling the trigger of the rifle under his fingers. All the training and all the knowledge seemed to be boiling off like steam as he sensed the predatory beast approach. There was a coldness in the precise advance of the creature that gave Ozymandias his first taste of fear—

the acid-biting tinge in the back of the throat, the tightness in the chest as he drew breath, the tenseness in his hands, and the seeming lack of proper coordination of his fingers.

He wanted to rush to the cab of the 'crawler and wake his friend, but he knew that it was unwise to disrupt the regeneration process. After all, the thought flashed through him, this was not a dire emergency; it was only a curious animal approaching the camp. There was no certainty of danger; Ozymandias handled a weapon that would blow the beast into vapor with ease.

There was no need to be afraid.

And yet he most certainly was . . .

Something moved again at the crest of the plain. For an instant the thing was captured in silhouette against the night sky. It was a quadruped, long in body, a pointed snout. Perhaps a wolf or a cragar, he thought, waiting.

It raised its snout, testing the scents of the night, and then turned again toward Ozymandias. It advanced into the shadows with a casual, loping gait which suggested boldness and confidence.

Ozymandias could not wait any longer, and squeezed off a shot in the direction he calculated the beast to have advanced. There was a burst of light, a halo of orange with a center burn of bright blue as the bolt of energy struck an outcropping of rock and disintegrated it. In the instant of afterglow, he saw the beast, as though captured on film, crouched beyond the first explosion. Its eyes were wide, but not with fear, its mouth hanging open to expose the sawlike teeth and long fangs.

There came a scrabbling of claws in the dry earth as the thing sprang forward, and Ozymandias fired again, without aim or thought. Two beams pierced the earth ahead of him bursting aimlessly into the dirt.

Where was the damned thing?

Raising the rifle to fire again, listening to the onrush of claws, the panting breath of the beast, Ozymandias fought the panic which rose in him like a column of white heat.

His breath was expelled from him from the force of the blow as the beast thudded into him. Knocked from his feet, his ribs crying out from the concussion, he struggled to draw a breath and felt his mind go white from fear as the impression of suffocating enveloped him. Time seemed to be stretching, elongating so that each second seemed an hour and he was of two minds as he watched *and* felt his reactions to the attack.

There was a great weight upon his chest, and the thing's snout was routing into his clothing, trying to find purchase for its fangs. Its breath was ragged and smelled like rotten meat, its claws raked at him as he pushed the stock of the rifle upward in vain attempt to lever the beast away from him.

I'm going to die.

The thought raced through him with an icy finality. There was calmness about the thought, which astounded him as much as it stirred him into action.

He *would* not die now. He could not allow it. He had not come so far and yet done so very little to be torn apart by a mangy, foul-smelling beast.

His jump suit was being split open like a piece of fruit and he knew that his chest would give way to the thing's claws just as easily. His training could not fail him now, and he summoned up the power of his mind which he knew lay waiting just beyond the threshold of consciousness.

His genetic engineering had been planned by his computerself, and the contingencies for psychokinetic ability had been a part of his initial body blueprinting. Ozymandias stared up into the eyes of the beast, into the dead-yellow pools, and imagined the small brain which labored behind them. He imagined his own mind extending an invisible hand—a strong, capable hand, with such strength that no force existed which could stop it.

Extending his invisible hand into the depths of the skull, he carefully groped about, trying to feel the pulpy, soft lobes. The beast clawed him again, and the wound in his chest threatened to distract him as he grappled with the loose folds of fur and flesh about the animal's neck. But his third hand kept moving, feeling, touching until it came upon the target—the unprotected dural layers, the slight convolutions, and the bulbous lobes of the lycanthic brain.

He touched the brain, felt it slip into the grasp of his telekinetic hand, and he slowly made a fist, squeezing the soft, gray mass into an undifferentiated soup.

Instantly the limbs of the wolf grew rigid and its jaws locked open. Its wide eyes grew wider still and its throat rattled with a night-piercing cry. Its back straightened as every nerve in its body recoiled from the final message, the final sensation which burned through the muscle and bone.

As Ozymandias withdrew his third hand from the ravaged skull of the wolf, he rolled to the side and the creature fell away from him. It smelled of death and was now among the dead itself. Eyes still open, mouth agape, it stared up toward the moon as though asking how this fate could have been possible.

The slash in Ozymandias's chest was not as deep as he had imagined, and he sealed it with a regenerative tissue balm from his ration pak. There was little loss of blood, and he would suffer no ill effects from the attack.

His breathing slowly calmed and his hands had stopped their trembling; he fought the backwash of adrenaline that now coursed through him. Standing in the moonlight over the body of the creature, Ozymandias paused to experience what had taken place, and tried to engrave what he was feeling in his memory.

He had killed.

Taken the life of another living thing. A half hour before, that lump of fur and sinew had been animated, moving, breathing, racing across the earth. And now it lay lifeless at his feet. There was a feeling of power and of loss within him. He wondered for a moment what kind of passage had been completed. From the light of awareness, where had the mind of the beast fled? To the nothingness of nonexistence, said his rational mind, and he railed against the idea for an instant. How was it possible to have *life* and then suddenly *not* have it?

The mystery seemed so simple, so foolish, and yet at the same time profound.

Ozymandias had truly joined the race of humanity. He had achieved his initiation, his calling card. He had killed.

CHAPTER 5

When Kartaphilos and Ozymandias reached the outskirts of Eleusynnia, it was decided to leave the 'crawler under camouflage and complete their journey into the city on foot. The appearance of the First Age vehicle would draw too much attention to the two travelers and could immediately place them under a wealth of suspicions. Kartaphilos felt that his companion would fare much better as an inconspicuous observer of the ways of humankind than as an unwilling participant.

Dressed in the flowing robes of wilderness sojourners, the pair entered the city, and at once Ozymandias fell under the spell of the magical city. Long accustomed to bleak interiors of the Citadel, the barren waste of the desert, and the Ironfields, Ozymandias was immediately awash in the sensual waves of the city. There were lights, colors, and sounds. Impressions and images, all brawling for his attention. They entered a long aviennza, where the vendors stalls were packed cheek to jowl, and the wind flapped at their rainbow tents and banners. The crowds were thick here and the air was shot through with the scents of spices, flowers, broiling meats and fishes, and the warm, pungent odors of laboring bodies. Accents and dialects peppered Ozymandias's ears and he struggled to differentiate the sounds, to make sense of the words.

Wagons and carts, pulled by all manner of beast and man, clogged the street, while the citizenry sifted for wares, haggling for prices, displaying their love of business and barter.

A small clutch of street musicians played stringed instruments and reedwinds at the end of the marketplace, and Ozymandias paused to listen to the keening fifth-note discordance of their specific tune.

"You can know that all this exists," he said to Kartaphilos, "But there is no substitute for experiencing it."

"No, that is certainly true."

They stopped at a stall where an old woman stood roasting broca nuts. Kartaphilos bought several, passed them into the hands of his friend, who relished their flavor as they continued to walk through the winding side streets of Eleusynnia. Ozymandias began to take special notice of the women, who in these quarters of the city were dressed in the native costumes of their traveling trader-husbands and escorts. There were the flowing gowns of the Odonians, the heavy-furred pelts of the Shudrapurs, the baubleflecked doublets of the G'Rdellians, and the skimpy kinis of the concubines and dancers. There were women of all complexions, heights, and weights. Black-haired, blond, shaven, and everything in between, the women walked and labored with their men. They were of all ages and ageless at the same time, and they were all fascinating to the young Ozymandias.

"There will be plenty of time for that sort of thing," said Kartaphilos.

"*What* sort of thing?"

"You could not be more obvious, my friend. Your eyeballs are almost leaping from their sockets."

Ozymandias laughed. "You don't understand . . ."

"Oh yes I do. You forget that once, albeit a long time ago, I was once a normal lad of sixteen."

Ozymandias looked away from him, and back into the

crowds, his eye settling fleetingly upon a young red-haired servant girl, who could not be more than sixteen herself. She wore a simple white tunic which clung to her young breasts and fell away from her milky-white legs as though she posed for an artist's brush.

"What are they like?" he asked as though in a trance.

"They are like you and me, and they are totally different. Do you remember something called *Madame Bovary?*"

"Early First Age fiction. Flaubert. Yes, of course, I recall it. Why?"

Kartaphilos shrugged. "Some say that it is one of the most incisive investigations into the mind of a woman ever written by a man. There are others who claim the honor should fall to a writer called Lawrence. No matter really, except that few men ever seem to come close to explaining with gentle susurrations."

"In other words, you cannot tell me what they are like."

Kartaphilos nodded. "I suppose. It seems that they are similar and different to all of us, but in never-ending variations. Don't rush into their special world without thinking, my friend. You will be lost in a wilderness."

Ahead of them walked a woman dressed in tightly sewn leggings and a leather vest. She carried a large knapsack filled with dried meats and fish. There was a hypnotic, swaying motion to her gait, a liquid movement that was so unlike the rocking, herky-jerky gestures of a man walking. There was a confidence and a poise, a grace that was altogether captivating. Poor Ozymandias was so unused to the physical reactions he was feeling that he had difficulty interpreting what his body was trying to tell him.

When he tried to explain this, Kartaphilos only laughed and claimed that eventually he would be more comfortable with his lust.

They left the marketplace and passed through one of the great cantilevered gardens and parks for which Eleusynnia had been long famous. Here the crowds were thinner and less furious. The air was sweeter and the colors more subdued although no less beautiful. Trees crowded one another for sunlight and the shade from their branches dappled the meadowlike lawns and pathways. Great fountains and reflecting pools accented the gardens and filled the air with gentle susurations.

As the pair cleared a hedgerow maze filled with topiary, they came upon a small crowd gathered in a clearing. There was a platform and a small, wrinkled man was standing before that gathering. He leaned upon a gnarled staff and spoke in a high-pitched voice that was a combination of age and enthusiasm.

"What's this?" asked Ozymandias.

"A public forum. It is not uncommon on any afternoon to come to the parks and find orations taking place in every open meadow."

"What do they talk about?"

"Whatever strikes their fancy—or irritates their spleen, as the case may be. Sometimes it's just a sideshow, sometimes it can be a meaningful discourse."

"Let's see what this old fellow's all worked up about." Ozymandias walked slowly to the back of the handful of people standing on the lawn watching the gray old man.

At first it was difficult to grasp the thread of the speaker's main theme. He rambled on about the diversity of political thought in the countryside, and the World in general, claiming that the only true solution was a banishment of all nationalism to form a truly unified World State. To all of this digression Ozymandias listened with amused tolerance, watching the crowd, and weighing their reactions to the old man's words. The general feeling from the listeners was a mild interest which could quickly drift toward apathy, given the proper stimulus in that direction.

". . . and it is a known fact now," said the speaker,

"that the myths about the First Age are nothing more than the cleverly planted lies of conspiring World leaders. It is obvious why the masses must be constantly fed the legends of the World before our own . . . so that all the seats of power have excuses for being the miserable failures that they are in governing our present modern world.

"First Age! A fabrication, I tell you! There *was* no First Age. We are living in the *only* age. I tell you . . . *We* are the First Age! And if there is to be any greatness in us, then we must demand it of our leaders, our taxmen, and our aldermen and dukes! Make *us* great, we must tell them! Make us *all* great!"

There was a spattering of applause and a few clearings of throats in the small crowd as the old man paused to draw a breath and see if there would be any lucid commentary from his audience. Just as he was about to continue, Ozymandias spoke:

"Only a fool would say there was no First Age," he said in a level voice.

The crowd had been quiet and save the eternal rush of nearby fountains, his words carried unhindered over their backs and to the ears of the elderly speaker.

"What's that, young man? You dare call me a fool?"

"You or anyone else who would believe what you are saying."

A murmur went through several of the listeners. A few turned to see who had spoken against the old man.

"Do you know who I am, you young sapling?"

"No, sir, I do not . . ."

Kartaphilos jerked upon his sleeve and whispered in his ear to stop the conversation before it became too late, but Ozymandias would hear none of it.

The old man tottered up to the front of the platform, holding his gnarled staff, touching his sunken chest. "I am Praxto the historian. I taught for almost three generations at the University of Nestor! How dare you contradict my words? I have seen a thousand young minds like yours. You speak from your glands, not your soul, and most certainly not your mind!"

Ozymandias smiled. The old man was no fool, that was for certain.

"You are a historian?" asked Ozymandias. "And what is history? What makes it so sacred, Praxto? Someone once said that 'History is but a fable agreed upon.'"

" 'Tis no fable, son. What is your name?"

Kartaphilos nudged his shoulder, but he spoke loudly for all to hear. "My name is Ozymandias."

There was a pause as the crowd and Praxto absorbed the name. Kartaphilos held his breath, hoping that there was no one among them who might recognize the name.

"That's an odd name, young one. From whence do you travel here? Zend Avesta?"

Kartaphilos nudged him again, and Ozymandias smiled. "Yes, yes, that's correct. I am from Zend Avesta. How did you know?"

"The name sounds like something the Avestans might use. But you are diverting me from my first objective. You say there was definitely a First Age and I say it has been a purposely constructed myth to explain away the failures of the World. Defend yourself!"

"I need no defense, Praxto. Have you traveled this planet? Have you ever gone beyond the small pitiful borders of this continent which we so presumptuously call 'the World'?"

"What difference does such a thing make?"

Ozymandias laughed and strode through the crowd to stand face to face with his opponent, leaving Kartaphilos in the background. "Oh, it makes quite a difference. Have you ever walked through the Manteg Depression at night? There is not a light nor a dwelling nor sign of human habitation for thousands of kays . . . and yet there are places in the earth where the ground still glows like phosphorus through the darkest hours, places where so many bombs exploded that their poisonous radiation still lights up the sky."

"There is no such place." Praxto folded his arms and looked to the crowd for approval, but they remained silent, all eyes upon the young dissenter.

"Oh, but there is. I have spoken with men who have been there, who have seen what I describe."

"There is no such man."

"Tell that to the famous Stoor of Hadaan. Surely you have heard of him?"

A harsh murmur coursed through the crowd. There were those among them who indeed knew of Stoor and his fabled exploits.

"You have seen Stoor? You know him?" someone shouted out.

Ozymandias nodded.

"Liar!" cried Praxto. "You are not old enough to have known such a man!"

Ozymandias smiled. "I am older than you think, old man. Older than you can imagine."

"You mock me, Ozymandias. It is disrespectful."

"It is disrespectful to walk to ends of the World and stare upon the Slaglands? Have you seen them, Praxto?"

"No, nor has any man."

Ozymandias laughed. "Thousands, perhaps millions, of square kays of glazed-over rock and earth. Stretching as far as the eye can see. A place where something so powerful simply leveled every topographical feature, melted it, and re-fused it as it cooled into a plain as cold and clean and empty as a glass tabletop. The Slaglands, Praxto. They exist, and have existed for millennia. The gravestone for the First Age! Do we have the power to do such a thing?

Have we ever conceived of any weapon or process so terrible? I tell you we have not, nor will we at any time in the foreseeable future. But there were those humans who came before us, humans who possessed the knowledge and power to control the fury of the sun itself.

"And what of the artifacts? The ruins of their cities we have found beneath the strata? The machines, and the pieces of equipment that explorers and soldiers of fortune sell to our museums?"

Praxto shook his head and smiled. "They are nothing more than clever fakes, my son. Have you not the wisdom to see such a thing? Nothing more than artfully contrived geegaws and gimcrackery."

"You *are* a fool," said Ozymandias. "Go to the Ironfields and look upon the works of First Age. Even in decay, in death, in corruption, you can feel the greatness that once rose up before us. We are but the handful of survivors of a once mighty race. Go to the Ironfields and gaze upon the greatness. Go, as I have gone!"

Another murmur passed through the crowd, and Ozymandias felt a rush of excitement as he sensed the power, the control, he carried over the crowd.

"You have seen the Ironfields?" asked an old woman to his left.

"Yes, I have traveled its length and its breadth. I have seen the bones of men who stared in the face of Armageddon."

"Where is this place?" asked someone else, a dark man with a carefully trimmed beard and a neat uniform, which Ozymandias could not have known was that of the militia.

"South of G'Rdellia, east of the Samarkesh Burn and the Republic. Beyond that, there are no exact coordinates. If one travels long enough, and looks hard enough, he will find what he looks for."

"How did *you* find it?" said Praxto.

"I met Stoor of Hadaan. He is rather intimate with the place."

"They say that Stoor is dead now," said a man near the front of the crowd, which Ozymandias noticed had easily doubled in size since he had come to the front of the platform. "What do you know of this?"

"I would be greatly saddened to learn such a thing. He was very much alive when I saw him last."

The crowd giggled to relieve the tension that was building among them. Ozymandias relaxed his mind and allowed the general sense of the group's feeling to wash over him. It was a low-level telepathic "read" of the crowd, a technique over which he had only now begun to realize that he had control. It excited him to finally know that there lurked within him still untapped powers and abilities, waiting only to serve his purposes.

His general impression of the crowd was favorable, and he felt that there existed within their minds a tinge of fear, some definite respect, and even admiration for someone with the nerve to speak out against the pyrotechnics of Praxto.

"Talk has been our cheapest commodity," said Praxto, breaking the silence. "You can make statements all day, and never have a frouna of proof."

"Proof will be at hand for all to see, Praxto. This is but the beginning of what will some day be called, perhaps, 'the Enlightenment.'"

"You speak like a prophet," said another from the crowd. "Is that your intention?"

Ozymandias smiled. "Not necessarily. Nor exactly. It is just that I believe we, as a race, have much to learn about our origins and our current condition. If I may be of service to all of you, then I will share in the general cultural and historical education of us all."

"Tell us more!" said a young woman.

"Educate us *now,* Ozymandias," said another man.

"More!"

Ozymandias raised his hands, staring briefly at Praxto to seek admission that he had indeed won over his crowd. The old man turned his back on him and cast a despising, single glance at the crowd before departing.

Ozymandias looked out into the crowd, feeling their curiosity build, sensing the excitement they broadcast like small children. "Have you ever heard of aircraft that fly by the power of the sun? Or potions you can drink that will prevent you from falling prey to any disease? To keep you from having babies? To make sure that you *do* have babies? What about growing vegetables as heavy and as tall as a man, and three times as succulent as anything you'll ever see in a vendor's stall? What about a machine that thinks, that could give you answers to any question? Can these things be?"

"No! You talk of magic, of sorcery!" someone shouted. "Not in this World, young one!"

"No, you are correct," said Ozymandias. "Not in this World, but in the past, in the First Age, the things I tell you of were child's play. I speak not of magic but of science."

As Ozymandias continued to discourse with the crowd, Kartaphilos hung back near its outer fringes, feeling ambivalent about the performance. There was a charismatic quality about his charge which he had not realized existed. The young man had a facility with the people that was almost frightening. And yet Kartaphilos wondered if it was a wise thing to give Ozymandias his head so early, to allow him to attain a high profile in a world of ignorance and misunderstanding.

It was true that the crowd was comprised chiefly of peasants, laborers, domestics, but there might be those among the crowd who would report back to superiors of keener minds, to those who would take a more special interest in the ramblings of a dashing young traveler, a seemingly harmless young soldier of fortune whose main asset was braggadocio. And there was something admirable in the way Ozymandias addressed his audience. He exhibited a boundless energy, a confidence, and an enthusiasm that was charming, hypnotic, almost heroic in proportion. He had the qualities needed to be a leader of men—a distinction that would be held in esteem in some circles, in contempt in others.

Kartaphilos vowed that he would watch closely for signs of either reaction brewing in their midst, no matter where they might be traveling.

He stood at the edge of the crowd for the better part of an hour before he caught the attention of Ozymandias. He signaled to him by subtle gesture of hand, and hoped that his charge would recognize his desire to leave the place. The young speaker smiled, nodded slightly, and fielded several more questions from the audience. Slowly, expertly, he handled the crowd, gradually tapering off the performance and implying that his stint upon the stage was almost at an end. There was no abruptness in him, no lack of understanding for the feelings of the crowd. He seemed, to Kartaphilos, to have an innate sense of how to handle them.

Presently he descended the platform to a sustained burst of applause and joined Kartaphilos. As the crowd melted away Ozymandias looked at his companion and smiled.

"I'm a bit dry. Shall we stop for an ale or some wine?"

Kartaphilos nodded, motioning them to walk toward the nearest avenue. "All right, but tell me something—why did you do that?"

"Ah . . . you disapprove, don't you?"

"I'm not sure yet. Tell me your reasons, though."

"Something bothered me about the way that old man could foist his nonsense on the people. I mean, you and I both know that he is wrong. What is wrong with educating the people?"

"Nothing at all—provided that they want to be educated. As you well know, a little knowledge can be a dangerous thing."

They edged along a crowded sidewalk until they came to a tavern called the Black Wing, where Kartaphilos pushed back a heavy oak door.

"I don't see anything dangerous in telling them about the First Age. It might get them up off their asses, get them moving again."

"You sound so naïve sometimes," said Kartaphilos as he walked to the closest unoccupied table, seated himself, and gestured for his companion to do the same.

The tavern was more than half filled with patrons, mostly men who were refreshing themselves from their day's work. There were docksiders, fishermen, roadmen, and traders, and no one seemed to be paying any particular attention to the two new arrivals.

"You know that I am *not* naïve. I may still be a bit inexperienced at being a part of this human race, but I am as wise as any man."

Kartaphilos laughed as he signaled for the barmaid. "That, unfortunately, is not saying a whole lot."

Ozymandias ignored the comment, started to speak, but waited until after the young woman appeared and took their order of two flasks of wine. Even though Kartaphilos had no need for the liquid, his artificial body would be able to process the wine, and later eliminate whatever could not be drained off as fuel for its minireactor.

The young woman returned with the flasks and smiled at Ozymandias. Her hair was long and golden, tied into two ponytails, and her brown eyes were bright and penetrating.

She was obviously admiring of the young man who sat with the robed, bearded one.

"My name is Heedne," she said. "Please call for me if you would like anything else."

"Why, thank you," said Ozymandias. "I will do that, indeed."

As she disappeared into the mist of smoke and barroom conversation, Ozymandias watched her.

"What did she mean by that remark?" he asked his friend.

"Hard to tell. It's not uncommon for the maids of such establishments to perform favors for the customers."

"You mean she is a common whore?"

Kartaphilos shrugged. "She looks fairly *un*common to me. Most of them are far less attractive."

"Should I ask her for some of her favors?"

"I don't think it works like that. Listen, my friend, there will be plenty of time for all of that. You have only today reached civilization. Be patient. Relax, and talk to me."

Ozymandias remembered then that he had been ready to tell his friend about the telepathic, almost empathic, reaction he had felt while talking to the crowd. He related this experience, and tried to re-create the feelings of one under the impress of psi powers. He said that he felt it was possible, with the proper training, to employ his psychogenetic abilities to far greater uses, and that here in the midst of the common people would be an excellent place to experiment.

"What are you talking about?" asked Kartaphilos.

"It is possible, you must realize," said Ozymandias, "to be able to perform psychokinetic operations—much in the same way as I killed that plainswolf, only much more delicately, of course. It is something that may be of great use to me, and I must practice; I must use my talents to their fullest."

"Yes, I agree. But all in good time."

Ozymandias nodded, although fully agreeing with his companion. They sat for a while in silence sipping their wine and admiring the lovely Heedne as she darted between tables to deftly serve and smile. Ozymandias wanted her with the youthful frenzy of an adolescent, although he labored under none of the ignorance usually associated with such callowness. His textbook understanding of physiology and a millennium's worth of erotica locked within his memory would serve him well whenever his chance came; he only wanted to turn theory into practice.

He was about to speak to Kartaphilos once again about the possibility when there came a sudden commotion at the other end of the tavern. A large man dressed in the furs of a herdsman, stood up and back from his table brandishing a curved handknife. Shouting something indistinguishable at another herdsman across the table, the large man lunged forward with his knife.

The tables about the two herdsmen emptied in an instant while everyone outside of the danger radius looked on with detached interest. The second man reached for his own weapon, but was a moment too slow. Before his knife was halfway from his sheath, the larger man's blade sliced neatly across his arm, severing arteries and veins. Blood erupted fountainlike across the table, and as the wounded man looked with stunned expression at the damage, the larger man attacked again, driving his blade deep into the man's shoulder, very close to the carotid arteries of the neck.

At the same time, the front door to the tavern burst open and a small detachment of militia zeroed in on the fray, two of the policemen quickly subduing the attacker with deftly applied yan-du martial strokes. At this signal, the tavern crowd broke ranks and surrounded the fallen, bleeding man.

"Incredible!" said Ozymandias, just as the action ended. "So fast! I can't believe it. Come on, let's see if we can help."

He started to rise from his seat, when the capable grip of Kartaphilos held his forearm. "Perhaps we should stay out of this . . ."

Ozymandias shook himself loose. "No! There's a man badly wounded. He might be dying."

As he drew closer to the ring of people about the victim, someone turned and asked if he was a surgeon. Shaking his head, Ozymandias told him that he was not, but that he knew some simple doctoring. No one tried to stop him as he bent low and cradled the man in his arms. The forearm cut was already closing, the blood starting to coagulate; the one above the shoulder was not faring so well.

Lifting up the furred cloak, Ozymandias saw that the knife had plunged deeply into the man's chest and had probably entered one of the main arteries leading away from the heart leading up toward the head. Although there was little exterior blood loss, he suspected internal hemorrhaging of a high degree.

"He's a goner if you ask me," said someone. "Look at his lips and his hands turnin' blue."

"Ain't no use with that one, Doc," said another voice.

Ozymandias knew that even the tavern folk would be right if something was not done quickly. The police had summoned a doctor, but there was no guarantee that he would arrive in time to help. Slowly, screening out the distractions of the tavern, Ozymandias imagined his hands penetrating the chest cavity, groping silently about the organs until the damaged area could be found. As he did this, the low rumble of conversation grew softer, and everyone was suddenly watching this handsome young man lay hands upon the body of the dying man.

In his mind, he could feel the hot, slippery wetness of the

chest cavity, the tough, rubbery tubes of the vena cava, the pulmonary aorta, and the neat slice of the damaged vessel. Summoning up energies as yet untried, he imagined the cells and tissue of the vessel, conjured them into movement and direction, and began restructuring them as a child might fit together a set of building blocks. The act became more clear the longer it was imagined, and gradually Ozymandias could feel the pulsing, shock-trauma fibrillation of the damaged body begin to cease. The healing had taken place; the man would not die.

As he removed his hands from the wound, he could see that it had closed, and as if by magic had begun to seal itself, already puckering up with new, pink flesh, the line of scar already diminishing.

Although he covered it quickly with the mangy, fur cloak, those of the inner circle of the crowd were not fooled. Shouts of amazement shot through them. Cries of "Healer!" and "Wizard!" were intermixed with exclamations of a darker hue. As Ozymandias stood and announced that the man would live, taking note of the flush in his hands and face, he noticed that the men in the tavern were backing away from him. Reaching out his mind to them he could sense their fear.

He withdrew his mind, fighting off the acid-tinged revulsion that was building in their minds. He was about to say something that might calm them when the door again flew back upon its hinges and the doctor arrived with a scurrying assistant. They pushed past Ozymandias and began to examine the victim, who was now resting peacefully, eyes closed, breathing normally.

Suddenly he felt a familiar grip on his shoulder and, looking up, saw the face of Kartaphilos staring at him from beyond the shadows of his hooded robe.

"Come. We must leave immediately!" he whispered.

"But—"

The grip became more forceful, vising down on his shoulder and lifting him to his feet. "Now!" hissed Kartaphilos, and pulled him through the crowd to the door in a swift, graceful movement.

"Wait!" someone cried. "There he goes! Stop them!"

"He's the one! At the park this afternoon."

As they cleared the door there was the sound of scraping wood and the rustle of boots upon the stone floor. The police and several of the crowd had begun the chase, and Kartaphilos broke into a run as they entered the street. The pedestrians regarded their flight with mixed interest and diffidence, and they cut left into a small alleyway filled with shadows and refuse.

Ozymandias slumped against a stone wall and looked at his companion. "What's going on?"

"You are creating what is known as a 'stir.' The local authorities will now be on the lookout for us."

"But why? We've done nothing wrong . . ."

"Doesn't matter. You have drawn attention to us. You are some kind of odd character to the people, and you have captured their interest. People will want to know *who* you are."

"But it was only a handful of men . . . a small group in the Gardens . . ."

"Ah, you must know the power of a rumor, my friend. And where is there a better place to begin the word of mouth? By now, they are probably spreading tales of you discussing and refuting the Cathadonian Mysteries, and practicing levitation on a dead man at the Black Wing."

Ozymandias exhaled slowly. "Surely you exaggerate."

"No, but I'm sure all the fine folks will have no trouble in doing so . . ."

"All right then, what do we do now?"

"Isn't that obvious? We leave this part of G'Rdellia immediately."

"Shouldn't we wait until nightfall?"

"Yes, of course. I meant under cover of darkness." Kartaphilos looked about the alleyway amid the boxes and crates of garbage. "I would suggest you find some trash that looks most comfortable. We have several hours before sunset."

Ozymandias settled in behind a large freight package overflowing with excelsior and vegetable cuttings. "What happens if they find us?"

"Depends upon the hour. If the streets are still crowded and it grows darker, we might want to fight them off and make a break for the 'crawler. With my superior strength and combat techniques and your own untested powers, I think we should be able to stand off a fairly large complement of ordinary men . . ."

Ozymandias smiled.

"What's so amusing at a time like this?"

"It's just something you said: 'ordinary men.' I suppose we are different from most of them. We are certainly not ordinary, are we?"

CHAPTER 6

They remained undetected until the sun fell beyond the spired rooftops of the city. To their disadvantage, however, Eleusynnia does not fall prey to the night as do many of the World's metropolitan sites. Known as the City of Light, it becomes aglow after dark with an extensive system of gaslit streetlamps and houselights. The system had been devised more than a century before by a famous architect and scientist who had discovered the remains of an immense underground storage vault. By an ingenious use of existing tunnels and conduits already in use for plumbing and waste disposal, the gaslamp system snaked through the underbelly of the city, making it one of the most beautiful evening sights east of the Aridard.

The illuminated avenues and boulevards were thus a blessing and a curse for Kartaphilos and Ozymandias. They departed their huddling place after dark in that hour where the merchants went home to warm dinners and the civil servant employed a change of shifts, when the day workers retired to their pubs and taverns, and the city changed gears for night running.

Avoiding the main thoroughfares, and resisting the temptation to become lost in the crowds of the entertainment districts, they slinked through backstreets, weaving a mazelike path through the southeastern quadrants until they reached the outskirts of the city itself. When they were within a quarter hour's distance from their vehicle, they noticed a small party of police, systematically fanning out across the neighborhood. Kartaphilos found it difficult to imagine that he and Ozymandias were the subject of so intensive a quest, and so was not terribly alarmed by the sight of the authorities. Most likely there had been a local disturbance of some kind and the men were out in search of the guilty parties.

"Just continue walking toward the end of the block," he told Ozymandias. "Chances are they'll take little notice of us—if they see us at all."

This was not to be the case, however.

"Excuse me, gentlemen," said a gendarme who walked up beside them, "but I must see some identification."

The policeman looked at them with a hint of wryness, as though he recognized them and was merely going through a necessary formality. He carried a small pikelike staff, which looked as though it could be used with great subduing facility.

"I'm afraid we have none," said Kartaphilos. "You see, we are travelers from Zend Avesta, and—"

Without finishing the sentence, the cyborg lashed out his left forearm with such force that the policeman's weapon was snapped in half as it dangled from his belt. The force of the blow jammed the man against the wall, where he collapsed in shock and pain.

"Let's go," rasped Kartaphilos, grabbing his friend's arm, as they ran toward the nearest shadows on the opposite side of the street.

Within seconds, the other police gathered on the scene to give chase; one of them piping on a small flutelike instrument which served to give their location to still others in pursuit.

Kartaphilos led his charge through the narrow streets which soon gave way to less residential roads leading out of the city and into the farming districts. Cutting across level fields, they chased their shadows in the moonlight while the police kept up pursuit.

"If we reach the 'crawler, we'll be safe!" cried Kartaphilos, leading the way through semidarkness.

Looking back, Ozymandias counted six men, only one of whom seemed to be gaining ground on them. He attempted to gather his psi energies to slow him up, but the adrenaline which rushed through him seemed to be blocking his concentration. He pondered this in quick flashes of thought as he ran, realizing that he still lacked the proper training, the familiarity of his powers to have full enough control over them. His encounter with the plainswolf had been a last-ditch effort, an act of almost unconscious desperation, whereas this simple flight apparently did not warrant such a final summoning of mental strength. He cursed his lack of experience as he ran to keep up with the mechanical, fluid strides of Kartaphilos, whose warrior-constructed body was serving him well in the emergency.

They reached a depression in the meadow which sloped down to the ravine where their vehicle lay under brush. Kartaphilos leaped upon the ladder leading up to the cab, and swung open the bubble door. As he keyed in the ignition switch, the machine whined, sparked into life. In another moment, Ozymandias was aboard, and the cyborg threw himself at the controls to jam the vehicle into lurching but powerful motion.

Kicking up roostertails of dirt and grass in its wake, the 'crawler accelerated away from the pursuers. Their speed increased until the machine rocked along at full speed, clearing small rises in the land, and thudding down into soft earth where its treads gouged long furrows into the ground.

"We made it," said Ozymandias, finally letting himself laugh as he looked back at the confounded policemen, now huddled together in a group on a faraway hilltop. In the moonlight, their silhouettes projected a sculpted image of dejection.

"For the moment," said Kartaphilos as he hunched over the controls.

"What do you mean? They can't catch us now."

"No, of course not—but I fear that our story will race ahead of us. We have lost our anonymity in G'Rdellia."

The 'crawler raced along through the moonlit prairie-land and neither spoke for several minutes. Ozymandias considered his companion's words thoughtfully. "It shouldn't really matter. We were just a pair of strangers—somewhat odd, but nothing all that odd."

"No," said Kartaphilos. "Think about it. A young man captures the attention and somehow the minds of a crowd while speaking in the Gardens; the people may be uneducated, but they can trust their *feelings,* their intuitions—they *felt* your power over them. Later that same day, the *same* young man heals a dying man, actually repairs a mortal wound in front of eyewitnesses. No feelings this time, but sensory evidence. When word reaches the authorities about this mysterious young man, he is seen escaping in a self-powered vehicle, the likes of which has probably never been seen by hardly anyone. Vehicles such as this 'crawler are known only to be in the hands of kings and dukes, presidents and sheikhs. They are the toys of the wealthy . . . No, my friend, we are *very* odd indeed."

"Then perhaps I was a young prince, out among his people. There are a number of explanations which would cover us."

"Try to tell the people that. They have always preferred the more exotic explanations for any mystery."

"Then what are we going to do?"

"It depends. We could put as much distance between us and G'Rdellia, as soon as possible. That way, the rumors would not precede us too quickly. We are heading vaguely east at the present. At this speed, we could reach Odo within a few days of hard travel."

"Odo sounds like an interesting place." Ozymandias smiled encouragingly.

"Or, we could sequester the 'crawler in the outlands near the Straits of Nsin, and book passage on a ship."

"A ship? Bound for where?"

"It doesn't matter. The closest port would be the Isle of Gnarra."

"Ah yes, the sorcerer's haven, is it not?"

"Well, it *is* a rather exotic place. Not many of the inhabitants would pay much attention to you there. At least on the isle, we would not stand out in a crowd."

"There is a disadvantage to that, however . . ." Ozymandias stared at the midnight-blue crispness of the sky.

"What's that?"

"The longer we stay huddled away on the Isle of Gnarra, the more time any rumors of our appearance in Eleusynnia will have to spread and grow out of proportion."

"So true. I suppose it is coming down to six of one, a half dozen of the other." Kartaphilos laughed.

"I've always hated that expression."

"So have I."

They looked at each other and laughed. It would be a long night of driving ahead.

By skirting several small villages and settlements that clung to the shires of the Kirchou River, which led into the Aridard by the Straits of Nsin, the two travelers were able to remain undetected. They also avoided contact with any of the well-traveled turnpikes and trade-routes, using the omniterrain capability of the 'crawler to its best advantage. There was an abundance of wild game in the plainsland leading to the river delta at Nsin, and Ozymandias used the opportunity to sharpen his psychokinetic skills as well as the lessons of memory on wilderness survival. He had already learned the value of practice over theory in terms of keeping one's own hide intact.

The sun was setting upon the jeweled crest of the Gulf of Aridard when they reached the escarpments of the Straits of Nsin—immense, sheer-walled cliffs which loomed above the crashing surf of the gulf. On each side of the river, the promontories rose up nearly five hundred ems. The 'crawler sat near the edge of the south scarp, at the base of what was believed to be some of the most awesome ruins of the First Age—the Guns of Kell.

Actually, the name of the place was misnamed, for there were no longer any actual guns, nor was there any place or nation or anything called Kell anywhere in the region of the Straits. However, there remained on each cliff two huge batteries, large carved-from-stone fortresses, which had obviously been ravaged by advanced weaponry. The trained eye could see where immense gun emplacements had once been installed for the obvious task of guarding the Straits of Nsin. On the southern scarp, the fortress had been violated badly, so that its upper regions resembled the shell of a broken egg. Its seaward face lay cracked and ruptured; massive black deposits appeared to have poured from the openings like molten lava or basalt, and then cooled, hardening into a meandering pattern. Kartaphilos said that the black slag was all that remained of the legendary Guns of Kell.

The scarp was a desolate place. It was a region where few men ever ventured. Nothing grew here in the poisoned ground, nor did any animals seek prey or shelter in its wind-swept heights. It was a perfect place to hide their landcrawler, and they left it within the concavity of a large crater, near the base of the fortress. From a distance, its ochre color rendered it almost invisible among the rocks and talus of the ruins—a natural camouflage.

Traveling down to the shores of the gulf on foot, Kartaphilos led his companion through a series of underground tunnels and passageways cut through the cliff side with a knifelike precision. Ozymandias knew that the First Age engineers had employed laser tools which burned perfectly round, structurally sound tunnels through the solid granite. The tunnels were still antiseptically clean, the emergency stairwells intact.

As they descended, there was an occasional evidence of past conflict, of death, and of desperation. The bones of men lay scattered upon several landings in the ancient stairwells, their configurations still showing the twisted positions of death which claimed them as they fell. Here and there were also the nests of small rodents and other huddling vermin, but there was nothing to suggest human habitation, discovery, or danger. The darkness was absolute within the shafts of the Kell installation, and only the electric torches of the two travelers kept them from being consumed in the hell-like blackness of the place.

After an interminable descent, they reached a landing from which a pinpoint of light flickered in the distance. Following a rugged subterranean path, they came to the exit from the emergency shaft. Although barely more than a fissure in the immense rocky crags at water's edge, the opening to the outside was large enough to permit their passage. Beyond a small foot ledge, the surf of the Aridard pounded out its endless rhythms. Slowly, they worked their way along the ledge to safer ground, then down steep slopes to a stony beach.

"There should be some fishing villages to the south. A few hours' walk, and we might be able to find a ship which will get us off the mainland," said Kartaphilos.

Ozymandias only nodded as he began following the old cyborg, whose prosthetic body functioned flawlessly and tirelessly like the machine that it was.

Hours later, the pair sat at a small tavern table with a fisherman named Karse—a small, dough-faced man whose features were as gnarly as briarwood, hands as weathered as a ship's prow. He spoke with a guttural, low-country accent which made him difficult to understand, but there was a dancing light behind his eyes which bespoke a slyness that should never be overlooked.

"Passage to Gnarra, eh? That's going to cost you," said Karse. "'Specially at this late hour. All the boats are in for the evening."

Kartaphilos nodded. "We can reward you well for your work. Tell us quickly now, will you do it?"

"What's the big hurry? You talk like fugitives, if you ask me . . ." Karse smiled to reveal an uneven row of teeth, long and darkly stained. "Maybe there's more in it for me for turnin' you fellows in?"

Without attempting to reply, Kartaphilos reached across the table with his right hand and grabbed the fisherman by the throat. The steely grip of his prosthetic hand hinted at the quick, crushing death that could be summoned in an instant, and Karse's expression turned from wily to terrified.

"Now listen to me," said Kartaphilos through gritted teeth. "You will either cooperate and be paid handsomely or you will die in an unpleasant manner. Remember where you are, fisherman: this a smelly, rotten little smear of a village. Men disappear in rough waters here every day. No one would miss you for very long. If you have decided to engage us, a simple nod of the head will do."

His features already showing the first signs of cyanosis, Karse managed to shake his ugly head in the affirmative, then quickly drawing his breath as Kartaphilos released his death grip from the man's fleshy throat.

"That's fine. We shall do business at once."

"Hey, look, mates, I was just kidding before," said

Karse. "Man's got to make a living any way he can. I'm sure gents like you can understand that."

"We only understand that we seek your service," said Kartaphilos. "If you instead give us a *dis*service, you will pay the consequences."

Karse swallowed thickly, avoiding the intense stare of Kartaphilos. "My boat's down the docks a ways. We can shove off now if you'd like."

Ozymandias smiled at the sudden cooperativeness and stood up to follow his companion and the fisherman from the dimly lit tavern. No one paid attention to their exit, and they moved through the rancid darkness to the slip where a small shallow-draft trawler lay tied to its moorings. Karse climbed aboard, yelling to awaken his first mate, and prepared to launch the small craft.

The passage across the moonlit waters was choppy and silent save for the creaking of the rigging and the flap of sails in the night wind. Kartaphilos stood in the aft section with Ozymandias, watching Karse and his mate as they maneuvered across the gulf waters toward the Isle of Gnarra.

"You were rather explicit back there, were you not?"

Kartaphilos shrugged. "It is all in knowing who you are dealing with."

"But how did you know he would respect you instead of pulling a knife or something like that?"

"Ozymandias, listen: you do not live as long as I have without becoming something of an astute judge of men. You learn quickly that there are all types of men, and that nobility is to be found in only a small fraction of any of us. The prime motivators are greed and power, and perhaps the pleasures of the flesh. Small places breed small men with minds smaller still."

"And Karse is one of those men?"

"You are learning, my friend," said Kartaphilos. "He

knew nothing of us, but he thought that intimidation might play in his favor. You see, the world is full of men like Karse. It is not their fault, but more that of the environment, which has shaped them to be survivors. A tough world insists that one be tough to survive in it."

"Are you trying to tell me something?" Ozymandias grinned as he kept his eye on the misshapen Karse, still bent over the helm.

"Of course! I'm *always* trying to tell you something. You said you wanted to learn about humankind, didn't you?"

"Yes, of course I did . . ."

"Then always pay attention to what I tell you. Not that I am always right, but at least I shall give you a starting point, a place of personal perspective from which you might launch your own feelings . . ."

"That makes sense. Go on."

Kartaphilos inhaled deeply of the sea air. "There is not much more to tell, actually, other than the example which Karse makes for others. You see, it is a sad fact, but very true: most men do not understand the language of logic, of fairness, of respect. They take your kindness to be weakness; your respect to be fear; your sensitivity to be an invitation to attack. In men such as this, you cannot allow yourself to be magnanimous; you must be able to face them on their own terms. You must get down in the muck and grapple with them; it is the only language they understand."

"It sounds so animalistic, so primal . . ."

"Yes, that is exactly what it is. You must always remember that the majority of humankind have very primitive perceptions of themselves and the World at large. They see none of the subtle interconnections among the various systems of the World. They are like children who are I-oriented, and cannot think of anything which does not affect themselves on a very direct and basic level."

Ozymandias looked out at the dark sea, flecked with moonlit whitecaps. "It seems so futile. Perhaps it was not such a good idea to wish to become a man . . ."

"Oh, no, it was a very *good* idea," said Kartaphilos.

"Why do you say that?"

"There is nothing better to become." The cyborg grinned. "Unless you want to become a cyborg. Live forever and all that."

"There's plenty of time for that. I want to explore the 'mysteries of the flesh' first."

"I can't blame you for that. You're quickly discovering that awareness is a completely new experience when it is contained by human tissue, is it not?"

Ozymandias considered the question for a moment, realizing how insightful his companion was. "Yes, and I have to admit that sometimes I feel like a child, as though I had never existed before you brought me to this body. It's as if all the centuries as Guardian never really happened. When I try to think back to memories of existence at that time, it is like a dream—a dream which grows more dim with each passing day."

Neither spoke for several minutes, before Ozymandias looked into the old eyes of his friend and mentor. "Tell me something: would you have killed that fisherman?"

"Without any compunction. Why?"

"I was simply thinking about that—the act of killing. You will recall how odd I felt after killing the cragar? I still wonder if I could actually kill another human . . ."

"Oh, yes, you could do it. Necessity has a way of making us do all sorts of terrible things."

"I suppose it does. It is a strange and terrible thing to be a man, isn't it?"

Kartaphilos looked at him thoughtfully. "Yes, it most certainly is, and it is about time you realized such a simple truth."

Ozymandias nodded slowly and turned his attention out to the dark waters. There were so many aspects of humanity that he did not yet comprehend, so many experiences still unfelt, that he doubted if he would be able to accomplish all that he wished to do in this eerie life he had chosen for himself. A chill passed through and he wondered if it was the coolness of the sea air, or perhaps some deeper stirrings within his own soul.

Up ahead, rising up out of the night like the head of some silent sea creature, the volcanic peaks of Gnarra loomed. Soon they would be setting ashore.

CHAPTER 7

Imagine a chunk of anthracite embedded within a piece of rose quartz. Contrast. Figure and ground. The distinction between the two substances so sharp, so crisp and clearly defined.

So it was with the Isle of Gnarra when compared with the Gulf of Aridard and its attendant nations. The isle itself was ancient, both geologically and culturally. Cut off as it was from the geopolitical flows of the mainland, the isle evolved more slowly, clinging fitfully to the old ways like a harridan pulling her ragged shawl more tightly about her head. The Isle of Gnarra was all that remained of a volcanic eruption on the sea-bottom of the Aridard. Having risen up from the blue-green sea millennia ago, the isle remains a jagged, truncated cone of basalt, pumice, and infertile ground. Its serrated cliffs and natural spires became the lair of magicians, sorcerers, and other necromancers, their castles and dark dwellings hanging upon the promontories like predatory birds in their rookeries. Gnarra thus remained the final bastion against progress, technology, and enlightenment.

When Kartaphilos and Ozymandias reached its shores, having dispatched the wretched Karse with a handsome payment in Odonian silver, they slipped unnoticed into the shadowed streets of a small seaside village called Hern. They came to an inn and were received with indifference by the night clerk, and retired to their rooms. Of all the places where a fugitive might find respite and anonymity, Gnarra was perhaps one of the finest of refuges.

The reason for this is quite simple. The people of Gnarra are not concerned with the outside world—the petty squabblings of nations, the disputes of trades rights, the gross national products or the latest developments in travel or communication. They are a dark populace of hardy peasant stock, accustomed to living off the austerity of their rocky farms, the few items of trade from their ports, and the strength of their beliefs in the ancient ways. They are a self-contained race of mystical pragmatists. Their philosophies are strict, harsh if need be, and eminently fair.

And so it was that Kartaphilos and Ozymandias were able to remain upon the dark isle for an extended time, using the opportunity to study the ways of solitary, independent men and women. Try as they might to find news of or rumor about their appearance in Eleusynnia, no word ever reached them about the series of incidents. It was as though the people of Gnarra were not interested, or perhaps felt that the tales of the strange travelers were too inconsequential to be concerned with. The isle was under the firm political rule of five elders called the Council of Five, all avowed wizards of the ancient teachings, and skilled manipulators of legend, superstition, and their blood brother, propaganda.

It was during the stay in Gnarra that Ozymandias became fascinated with the age-old dichotomy of magic *vs.* science, and sought to investigate the phenomenon of the former, intending to discover what forces were at play, and why it seemed to work for those who wished it so. Against the desires of Kartaphilos, Ozymandias became associated with an old sorcerer named Beldamo, whose habit was to dine each evening in a small district tavern and perform tricks for the customers, to spin tales of magic and legend, and to generally divert the crowds. For this small attraction, Beldamo received a complimentary meal each night.

On one such evening, after listening with a certain amount of tolerance, Ozymandias approached old Beldamo and began asking him questions about the Ancients, about the Powers and the Seers, the Forces of the Eldritch Regions. The old sorcerer must have recognized the cleverness of the young man at his side, and soon warmed to his topics with enthusiasm, guarded with knowledge that his mind was being picked as cleanly as the bones of carrion.

After that first evening, as they prepared for the night in their quarters, Ozymandias told Kartaphilos his current plan. "How long do you feel we shall be on the isle?"

Kartaphilos shrugged. "Who knows? We have no timetable."

"Well, since you feel that way about it, I'm thinking of taking up with Beldamo for a short period."

"That old charlatan! What for?" Kartaphilos shook his head disgustedly.

"Because he is an interesting human being. He has that certain spark of charisma and difference that is sadly lacking in most. Besides, I would like to learn all that I can of this thing called magic . . ."

"Why?"

"Because I don't believe that it is *magic* at all, but rather an artfully concealed manual of control over forces that the technologists have simply overlooked. It is a body of knowledge which demands to be understood, rather than simply dismissed as mumbo-jumbo."

Kartaphilos nodded slowly. "Well, I can see your line of reasoning, I suppose. You are not the first to have imagined it thusly."

"No, of course not. My datafiles are filled with such speculations from First Age thinkers and scientists. There were even many experiments carried out with mystics, lamas, and other guru-type ascetics. I would like to observe Beldamo and perhaps learn what is actually going on in his tight little world."

"So, you shall become a sorcerer's apprentice?"

"For a time, yes."

And so Ozymandias toiled long hours in the dark rooms of Torrent Keep, the castlelike dwelling of Beldamo, which overlooked the village of Hern from the slopes of Mount Alb. In addition to access to many of the World's ancient secrets, Ozymandias also discovered access to the World's *most* ancient of secrets . . .

Her name was Miratrice.

Granddaughter of Beldamo, Miratrice was less than twenty but beyond the age of consent. To say that she was the most beautiful female Ozymandias had ever seen would have been the grossest of understatements. Her hair was a cascade of golden light, which fell across her marble-white shoulders in carelessly sculpted ringlets and curls. Her face was a perfect oval, accented by high cheekbones which emphasized her large fawn eyes, the color of a wet autumn afternoon. Her nose was thin and graceful, perfect and in harmony with naturally colored lips, full, sensual, and carrying the suggestion of a perpetual pout.

Miratrice.

She was at once a child and a woman. Her body was that of a Kiemer dancer—long and willowy, yet voluptuously curved, artistically sculpted as though from the mind of an aesthetic god.

It should be noted that by this time, having spent several months on the Isle of Gnarra before aligning himself with Beldamo, Ozymandias had lost his innocence (his virginity, if you will), through several fleeting encounters with tavern maids, flower vendors, and acquaintances of village ne'er-do-wells. These early sexual unions were of the simplest, most base kind: dark, perspiring couplings, filled with the urgency of dam-breaking lust, and concealed beneath the kaleidoscopic brilliance of novelty. Initially, Ozymandias lay fascinated with the physiological concepts involved, and he found difficulty in divorcing his thoughts from the functional aspects of coitus, thereby allowing his libido to simply *enjoy* each encounter. His curiosity and the manner in which he explored the mysteries of the female body were more those of the scientist, the philosopher, than those of a lover. It was only at the moment of climax that he would ever lose control of his rational explorations, and even then the moments were brief and, although ecstatic, in the final analysis, unsatisfying.

Unable to admit these subconscious feelings to himself, Ozymandias refused to recognize what it was in his relationships with women that was so obviously absent. His extensive memory and catalogue of facts pressed at his mind to verbalize his feelings of unfulfillment, but he would not allow it. Images of the great artists of the First Age, the playwrights, the sculptors, painters, and writers who had driven themselves to capture the essence of that special thing in humankind's kit bag of experience which set them apart from all other living things—the elusive thing called love.

Quite simply, Ozymandias had not the slightest inkling as to the true nature of love, and had even less of an idea as to where he might encounter it, or even recognize it when it was upon him.

Until, of course, there was Miratrice.

The first day he stood in the receiving hall, the great foyer of Beldamo's residence, he had not expected the company of anyone other than the old sorcerer. The shadows were long and heavy within the large room, and the musty smell of aged tapestries filled his nostrils. Beldamo welcomed with a grunting, unintelligible word, and gestured to him to follow him into the next room. The old man wore a baggy robe which had long ago lost its shape and any real color or design it may have once had. It hung on his gaunt frame like a gray shroud, which provided a very close match to his long silver hair and flowing beard— physical attributes that seemed to be *de rigueur* for wizards and their ilk.

As he followed the old man, he heard footsteps on the central staircase at the far end of the receiving hall, and turned quickly to see their cause.

A vision: gold and white and silk, set in motion by the lightest step, the most graceful of movements, the silent carriage of beauty and bearing. Miratrice descended the stairs with a natural, yet majestic demeanor that was altogether hypnotic to the young Ozymandias.

"My granddaughter, Miratrice," said Beldamo in his low, rumbly voice. "And this is my latest student, Ozymandias."

"Good afternoon, sir," said Miratrice. Her voice like the softness of a summer breeze.

"I—I had no idea that—" Ozymandias paused, struggling to find his voice, his meaning. "I mean, Beldamo did not mention that— No, I'm sorry . . . What I mean to say is that I am pleased to meet you."

Ozymandias stammered, haltingly looked down at his feet.

"Don't be embarrassed, lad, my Miratrice has a similar effect on all the young men when they first encounter her." Beldamo threw back his head and laughed in a rare expression of mirth.

"Grandfather, please . . ." Miratrice lowered her eyes and blushed appropriately.

Ozymandias stood for a moment, pulling back from the encounter to study it. It was as though he had been thrown into the most ancient of fairytales, and the utter unreality of the situation danced before him teasingly. It was as though he could walk away from the scene and it would have never existed.

But he knew that it was real, and that it was happening to him. It was the dreamy quality of the meeting with Miratrice which enthralled him. If he were to believe the wisdom of his memories, things like this did not happen in the dim, grim reality of the current World.

And yet it was real.

She was real.

"You have to believe me, and try to understand," said Ozymandias. "I've never met a woman like her. She's so different from any of the women I've ever known."

Kartaphilos laughed as he sipped some wine from a small goblet while they sat talking in the room at the inn.

"What's so amusing?"

"Oh, it is just that you are uttering lines of such prosaic intensity I would have never imagined hearing them from the likes of you."

"Prosaic intensity?"

"Yes," said Kartaphilos. "I would imagine that those selfsame words have been spoken by literally billions of men, billions of times, throughout the entire history of humankind."

"I can't help it . . . It's truly the way I feel about her."

Kartaphilos smiled and sipped again from his wine. "Oh, I don't doubt you for a moment. I believe that you are sincere. But tell me, does Beldamo know how you feel about his granddaughter?"

Ozymandias considered the question. "I don't really know. From the way he acts, he does not seem to care one way or another. His mind is operating on a different plane most of the time. He claims to be in tune with the frequencies of other dimensions, the places from which he draws upon his powers . . ."

"You don't sound like you believe him."

"No, of course not. He is what could be called an *adept,* I suppose. He is dealing with the powers of the mind almost exclusively. I don't know where he acquired his training or abilities, but he is well developed in the practice of psychokinetics, telepathy, clairvoyance, and all the rest. He is a psi, nothing more, nothing less; his whole grimoire of incantations, potions, and the like are mere crowd pleasers —although I expect that he believes them to accomplish what things he may do. The power of suggestion is strong in wizards."

"I'm not surprised," said Kartaphilos. "Listen, I am not trying to distract you from your discussion of Miratrice, but I *am* also interested in the initial reason for your sorcerer's apprenticeship."

Ozymandias waved him off with his hand. "No, no. That's perfectly all right. I understand. I think that actually, he had little to *teach* me that I don't already have an inkling about. What Beldamo is very good for, however, is the act of refining my own powers, and learning how to use them in all situations. I think I told you that I have been practicing levitation, and I'm getting quite good at it. Soon I will be able to actually propel myself through the air. Teleportation is something else again, and requires, if you are to believe Beldamo, long years of practice. I tend to agree with him. I can't do it."

"You've tried?"

"Oh, yes, on many occasions, but it is not working. I have the potential to do it, I'm sure. I can—I can *feel* that power inside. I know that it's there and I must just learn to control it."

Kartaphilos paused in his conversation, lost in thought for a few moments. He stared intensely at his companion, and there was a mixed expression of awe and intimacy. "You must realize," he said slowly, "that if you ever bring all your abilities to fruition, you will indeed be a superman . . ."

Ozymandias smiled. "Yes, I do. It is simultaneously a comforting and a disquieting thought."

Kartaphilos nodded. "Good. That is as it should be."

"You mean a little humility never hurt anyone?"

"Exactly. We don't want you getting delusions of grandeur, or anything like that."

"I don't think that will happen to me. I am aware of the problem, and therefore have an edge on dealing with it, if it ever arises."

Kartaphilos smiled again. "Yes, I am quite sure that you can. I must admit that I have been quite pleased with your progress. You have not only proved to be a good companion—something I've not had for a good long time—but also a fascinating person. Your curiosity is insatiable, and you seem to have acquired an altruistic nature that is most gratifying to someone like myself, who was created solely for the purpose of war and all its attendant agonies."

"It is a difficult business learning to be a man," said Ozymandias, "but I think I am doing a creditable job of it. Your encouragement is of great value to me."

"Yes, and aren't we getting formal on each other." Kartaphilos smiled again. "Now, go ahead, and tell me more of the beautiful Lady Miratrice. I can tell that you are fairly bursting to do so."

Ozymandias blushed slightly and laughed. "I thought you would never ask. All right, listen."

From the very first evening of their meeting Ozymandias had sensed a special attraction between himself and Miratrice. Initially, he was not surprised that it was primarily physical. After all, Miratrice was a ravishingly beautiful woman, and he was not unhandsome, conceit be damned.

But there was something which transcended their physical attractions for each other, and in the beginning, Ozymandias could only describe it as an extremely natural ability to communicate with ease and sincerity. Being the granddaughter of a sorcerer had its distinct advantages and therefore Miratrice was a marvelously informed, intelligent creature. She was worldly wise, and full of the necessary skepticisms and healthy attitudes required for survival in a harsh World.

Although his sessions with Beldamo were long and sometimes taxing, he looked forward to free time when he would meet Miratrice in the atrium of the Keep for tea, or perhaps an afternoon cordial. They spent every afternoon, during Beldamo's daily nap, talking in the garden, in the atrium, or on one of the parapets which overlooked the village below.

Ozymandias discovered that Miratrice was practically a prisoner within the Keep, because of Beldamo's distrust (admittedly well founded) of the village men. In his effort to protect her from the baseness of such men, he was also depriving her of her natural inclinations to company, warmth, and even sensuality. For the first few weeks of their meetings, Ozymandias thought it wise not to allow Beldamo to know of the growing intensity of his relationship with Miratrice. In order to avoid friction and misinterpretation, he felt it would be to advantage to first build up a feeling of trust and good will between Beldamo and himself.

This proved to be a good course of action, and eventually, when the old sorcerer began to take notice of the young couple, rightly interpreting the covert glances that came between them when together, it was old Beldamo himself who finally suggested that Ozymandias accompany Miratrice on short trips to the village, and perhaps a few day tours through the countryside, for, as the grandfather remarked, there was a quiet, haunting beauty on the isle which could not be found anywhere else in the World. One only had to know where to seek it out.

And so Ozymandias and Miratrice spent what seemed to be endless afternoons and early evenings exploring nearby regions of Gnarra's haunting country. They walked along the promontories of the Nighla Peaks, a rugged backbone of young mountains which ringed the eastern shores of the isle, where the ruins of ancient wizards' domains could still be found crumbling into talus on the treacherous slopes. Down in the villages they lost themselves in the color and splendor of the marketplace, testing the foods of the vendors, the winesellers, and the patisseries. A universe of sights and smells and tastes came to Ozymandias during these days, all accented with the warm touch, the gentle smile, and the lilting laughter of Miratrice. The impressions of the days were so vividly colored, interwoven, and commingled with his feelings for Miratrice that he felt he would have been incapable of enjoying them without her company.

They picnicked on the shores of the Aridard, watching the gulls feed and dive into the sea in breakneck drops, only to surface with a gullet of small prey. The wind touched their faces gently, and the occasional intrusion of a beachcomber or fisherman's boat was hardly noticed. Ozymandias was being consumed by the totality of the woman by his side, and he ached to lie with her in the endless night of passion and, yes, love.

It was not night when the final barriers were withdrawn, but the somber, shadowed darkness of afternoon in Beldamo's Keep. The wizard had recently retired for his afternoon nap, and Ozymandias flew from the ancient study to the upper chambers where Miratrice awaited him with a simple lunch of goat cheese, hearth bread, and plum wine. She was dressed in a long, flowing robe, which he had

never seen before, and he could only surmise that it was
not a dress but rather a dressing gown, a garment for the
boudoir and not the streets. Her hair fell away from her
face in abandoned curls and ringlets, giving her a tousled,
awakened, and ready-to-be-aroused appearance. They
dined in almost complete silence as he continued to stare at
her face, her body as it appeared beneath the transparent
folds of silk.

Miratrice too must have sensed the magic of their moment together for she respected the silence and remained a
blushing picture of contentment that the young man whom
she had grown to know and respect so well could be so
enraptured with her. Although Ozymandias suspected that
there was an element of plan in their afternoon tryst, he
could not help but lose himself in the building crescendo of
desire which surged through him.

Reaching out, he touched her hair, watched it fall across
her face. As she looked up at him, her large, wet eyes were
those of a helpless forest fawn. They spoke to him in their
helplessness and he knew that she asked for him to be
gentle. The robes fell away from both of them and they re-
joiced in a flow of touching, silence, and embrace.

For Ozymandias, it was the consummation of his desires
and his ideological notions of what love was intended to
be. For the first time in his short human existence, he felt
the organic flow of passion mingled with the soul-searing
heat of human caring, human sharing. Suddenly, in an instant of Zenlike *satori,* he was admitted to that inner chamber of understanding where love fuels the fire of the human
spirit. All the millennia of artistic outpouring, all the
poems, all the music, all the drama—it suddenly made
sense to him. It was the experience that would shape the
rest of his days, of that he was certain. Never before had he
imagined that there could be such capacity within himself
for such sharing, such unselfish caring . . .

Afterward, as they lay in each other's arms, neither could speak nor even look at one another. There was a common understanding of the importance of the moment for both of them, and there was no need to communicate it. Ozymandias himself felt suffused with a sense of completeness, of fulfillment, and that the elusive object of his quest was finally at hand. It was incredible to him how *clear* so many of the references to love within his datafiles now seemed. It was as though someone had removed an opaque veil from his face.

He looked up, and found that Miratrice was staring at him, her eyes deep and penetrating.

"I don't know much about this kind of thing," he said slowly, with a small amount of hesitation, "but I think that I love you very much."

She smiled and touched his forehead with the tip of her finger. "I am sure that I know less than you, but I feel that I am falling in love with you also."

As she said those words, Ozymandias felt his heart leap within his chest with all the clichéd strength of a lifetime of bad poetry—he knew what they had all been trying to describe, and damn it, it *did* feel like your heart was leaping!

He spoke her name over and over, repeating it as though it were the gentle lyrics of a song, and it seemed at that moment that her name was the most beautiful word he had ever uttered.

"What are we going to do?" she whispered, as though breaking out of a trance.

"What do you mean?"

"My grandfather—he would never permit this sort of thing. We must be married before—"

"Then we'll get married!"

"No, but you do not understand. It is the law of Gnarra

that a woman's guardian is responsible for the selection of her husband. Don't you see?"

"Beldamo seems to like me well enough," said Ozymandias, obviously not seeing the importance of her words.

"No, my love. That is not enough that he might 'like' you. He may think you are the finest young man in the nation, but you cannot be allowed to marry me . . ."

There was a grinding of emotions within his mind, anger and heartache, outrage and disbelief. "But why not! What are you talking about?"

Miratrice looked away, pulling the edges of the silk sheets about her breasts. She spoke as she looked past the curtains of her window, out at the sea in the distance. "Because the daughters of wizards are considered to be of royal blood, of special parentage here on Gnarra. They can only be wedded to someone of another royal family."

"Royal family?"

"The son of another wizard . . . don't you see?"

"Oh, I see it quite clearly, but that will have to be changed. Miratrice, I *love* you. I won't live without you."

"You will have to, I fear." She looked back at him. "Oh, my Ozymandias, what have we done? What is this terrible thing we have done?"

She started to cry, and feeling embarrassed turned away from him. He reached out to touch her shoulder, to give her comfort, and she flinched, drawing away from him.

"Don't touch me!"

Ozymandias grew quickly confused. How could she be so warm and full of love in one instant, and be so totally transformed the next? It was clear that there was much he still needed to understand about the deportment of women.

"Don't *touch* you? What do you mean?"

"It's wrong! We're doomed if we continue this. We should have never let it happen—"

"But Miratrice, it already *did* happen. We cannot deny our feelings, our bodies. We have loved and we *do* love."

"There is no hope for us; please, leave me now."

The last words stung him so sharply that he could not respond to them. Instead, he attempted a different course. "Besides, I have the answer to our problems."

Turning, she dared look into his eyes. "You do?"

"You said that it is law that you must marry a wizard, correct? Well, then, I *am* a wizard!" He tapped his chest lightly and smiled.

For a moment Miratrice stared at him, without expression, before suddenly laughing.

"What's the matter?" Again, Ozymandias was confused. Was it not only minutes before she had been crying fitfully, and now, as he attempted to console her, she *laughed?*

"Please, my love, do not try to make jokes. That will not help us."

"Jokes? I'm not making jokes! I am serious. I *am* a wizard, or at least I can be."

"Oh, Ozymandias, you don't understand. You are nothing but an apprentice. If Beldamo so chooses, he can cast you out, and you would never learn the Secret Arts . . . It would take you many long years to become accepted within the Enlightened Circle!"

He was not certain what she meant by 'Enlightened Circle,' but he did not really care. If only he could explain to her who and what he really was, and how he understood that her grandfather's powers were not all that special or secret after all— Well, perhaps he should try, he thought.

And he did.

"You told her *everything?*" asked Kartaphilos as he sat in the corner of their small inn quarters.

"Everything."

"And did she understand you? Did she really grasp the

concepts that you glibly tossed about? Cyborgs, Armageddons. Robots. Computers and Artificial Intelligence? Did she actually believe you when you told her that you had been created whole at the age of twenty-two, that you had no childhood, and yet you were millennia old?"

"Well, I must admit that quite a bit of it was something of a surprise to her."

Kartaphilos smirked. "Sometimes you have a marvelous gift for understatement, my friend."

"Oh, what I mean is that she had trouble picking up the concepts at first. But after I had explained each particular, she seemed to gain a fair grasp of what I was saying."

"And her reactions to all of this?"

"Quite surprising, actually."

"Meaning?"

"Meaning that she *believed* me. I mean, after all, I do realize it's a rather fantastic tale."

"And you feel that she believes you because she *wants* to believe you, is that it?"

"Well, that, and also that she is very much in love with me. I am sure that is a large factor."

"I am equally sure," said Kartaphilos. "Now, then, what did you tell her that you can do about this little dilemma? Does she feel that you can actually become a sorcerer or wizard or whatever?"

Ozymandias shrugged. "Of that she is not quite certain. Apparently love has its limits, and of course she is steeped in a mystic tradition that spans centuries."

"Did you give her a demonstration of your powers?"

"The thought occurred to me, but no, I did not. I could not imagine playing the equivalent of parlor tricks to that woman. It would have been somehow insulting, or demeaning, if you understand how I felt."

"I think I do. But go on. What do you propose next?"

"I think going directly to Beldamo and confronting him

on the topic would only infuriate him and alienate him. Mentors seem to loathe arrogant, boasting students. Instead, I plan to continue my studies, to meet with Miratrice, and to further attempt to understand all of these new experiences. When the time comes to inform Beldamo, I will recognize it."

And so Ozymandias had his plan well laid, only to discover that the schemes of men as well as rodents are often disturbed.

It was a somber autumn afternoon, while lying in the naked white arms of Miratrice, that Ozymandias recognized the time to inform old Beldamo.

More than simply *time,* but rather absolute necessity, since the old man was standing in the doorway to his granddaughter's bedroom, his gray eyes burning like lumps of charcoal.

Before either of the young lovers could speak, Beldamo released his pent-up rage, his indignation, and his fury. Amid cries of "Philanderer!" and "Swine!" and various other epithets, he raised his skeleton-thin arms and proceeded to wreak fairly conventional havoc about the room. Furniture and tapestries flew from their moorings, Miratrice's dressing table was overturned, and the curtains flapped furiously in an unfelt wind. Ozymandias could almost see the sparks flicking and jumping from the old wizard's fingertips.

Over the din of crashing fixtures and the inarticulate shouts of the old man's rage, Ozymandias tried to interject pleas to reason, and for a time to discuss the matter, but there was no stopping an outraged sorcerer.

It was only when Ozymandias felt himself being lifted unseen from the floor, gripped in the telekinetic forces of Beldamo, that he realized that there would be no talking until there had been a matching of strengths, of wills, and of purposes.

Summoning up his own powers, he imagined the hands, the invisible psychic hands of energy which gripped him. With the quick reflexes of survival instinct, Ozymandias extended his own telekinetic hands and grappled with those of Beldamo. It was the element of shock and the unexpected parry which gained him a brief advantage. So abrupt had been his defensive move that Beldamo had not been prepared, and suddenly the old man was wrenched from the cold stone floor and thrown out of the room.

As he crashed against the outer corridor wall, Ozymandias leaped naked from the bed to follow up his counterattack. Reaching the threshold, he saw that Beldamo had already gained his feet, renewed fury in his eyes.

"So, the young puppy thinks he can match his master, does he?"

"You don't understand, Beldamo. Things are not what they seem. I don't want to challenge you! Can't we talk about this?"

"The only speaking to be done will be over your grave, lad!"

"Grandfather, please!" It was Miratrice, having pulled on a dressing gown and standing behind her lover. "Please listen to him!"

"Stand away, harlot! Your father would have you staked for what you have done! I'll deal with you after I've disposed of this vermin who's invaded my Keep!"

Before anyone could reply a smoking bolt of light and heat struck the doorframe above Ozymandias's shoulder. A great chunk of stone fragmented and the entire lintel and post collapsed. Miratrice backed away as the rock crumbled, half sealing her into the bedroom with the ensuing rubble.

In the moment of the crash, Ozymandias tried to grasp the extent of the power of Beldamo, and attempted to discover what manner of force was being employed. His logic told him that if the energies were existent, and waiting to be tapped, he should be able to draw upon them as well as Beldamo.

If only he had studied a bit longer . . .

Another bolt of energy struck the stone wall by his head and he dove to avoid the exploding pieces. Reaching out with his mind he smacked Beldamo across the face, not with the purpose of harming as much as of distracting the old man from his appointed task. Beldamo reeled from the blow, losing his balance for an instant, giving Ozymandias time to scurry from the corner of the corridor and bound down the curved stairs to the receiving hall and the labyrinth of rooms below. He needed space in which to operate, time in which to think out his counterattack.

Clearly, he could not withstand a simple trading of blows with the wizard, for while they might—and his mind stressed the word *might*—be equal in strength, Beldamo had years of wily experience at his command. He would know all the tricks of the trade, and would not hesitate to use any of them.

As he rushed into the great high-ceilinged room which served as Beldamo's study, he heard a roar behind him. Turning he stared into the saucerlike eyes of the most hideous beast ever imagined. Huge and squat, it reared back on scaled haunches, peering down at him from a serpentlike neck. Its head was like a dragon's, yet vaguely human in appearance. Saliva streamed from the corner of its sawtooth mouth, and it expelled a foul breath which threatened to suffocate Ozymandias.

So stunned by the sudden appearance of the monster was Ozymandias that for an instant he stood transfixed by the sheer horror of the beast. When the thing did not immediately lash out with one of its front claws and rake him into ribbons, the thought struck him that it was all illusion. Many times he had seen Beldamo create small illusions, which were simply worked by implanting telepathically the suggestion of the vision in the subject's mind; then, after allowing the free-form images of the subject to fill-in the blank spaces, an illusion would invariably take shape.

Ozymandias tried to imagine from what nightmare this thing in front of him had crawled, but he grew convinced that there was no real danger.

Footsteps in the outer corridor and Beldamo appeared, smiling triumphantly. Staring at the old man, Ozymandias conjured up the image of a great war mech—a treaded, fighting robot, equipped with servo-arms and a variety of automatic weapons. These machines had been used extensively during the waning phases of the First Age to carry the battle to hostile environments, places where troops would have been at a distinct disadvantage.

Spurred on by the flood of adrenaline, the image burst into pseudo reality within the confines of the chamber, so tall and massive as to dwarf even the size of the dragon-beast. The war mech clanked forward slowly to engage the beast, and Ozymandias watched the smile fade from Beldamo's lips.

Lashing out, the scaled monster rasped its claws across the brushed-alloy finish of the war mech, doing no damage and making only the suggestion of a sound. It was ironic, and yet terribly fitting that the two illusions appeared in the forms that they did. How perfectly symbolic did the images represent the heritages of the two combatants, thought Ozymandias, although he realized that now was hardly the time to be thinking philosophically.

Summoning up his mental energies, Ozymandias imagined the fighting machine to extend its grapple arms and throttle the writhing creature, and it did so with instantaneous precision, at the same time lancing its ugly head with a tight beam of mazer-light. The beast wailed horribly as its skull blackened and smoldered, the once-green, scaly flesh dropping away in seared chunks.

Before the carnage could continue, the entire illusion disappeared in a blinding flash, leaving the machine of Ozymandias working violently at the empty air.

"So, you are not as harmless as you seem," said Beldamo, somewhat shaken by the power of his former student, but no less determined to destroy him. "What *are* you? *Who* are you?" he asked as if suddenly suspecting a dreaded deception. The old man's eyes brightened. "You are no student! *Blaeus!* Is it you!?"

Ozymandias stared at him strangely, suspecting a trick but trying to read the expression in Beldamo's face.

"Who is Blaeus?"

"Don't be so coy, my old friend, my rival! It *is* you, is it not? You've come back, somehow, and wish to avenge what you feel has been an injustice . . . Tell me that I'm right!"

Ozymandias shook his head. "No! No! I don't know any Blaeus. I am Ozymandias. Please, believe me!"

"Liar! Only Blaeus could equal me as you have done. It must be you, ancient enemy of mine!"

As Ozymandias began to reply, Beldamo seemed to be growing taller, then larger, growing rapidly into a towering giant. Another illusion, to be sure, but a terribly impressive one. Matching tricks had so far kept him apace with the powers of his opponent. *Time to get big,* thought Ozymandias, as he began to imagine the proper set of connections and images that would effect the feat. As he tried to *feel* what it would be like to actually expand in size, in the instantaneous moments of thought, he reflected upon the wisdom of his choice in having sought out the guidance of

Beldamo. If he had not tried to exercise the dormant powers, it might have been many years before he achieved the level of ability he was now employing. Add to that instruction the stress of the moment, and the old saw that necessity is indeed the mother of all invention.

Within an eyeflash, he stood towering above the fixtures of the chamber so that everything appeared to be like doll's furniture. He stared into the face of the equally large Beldamo and spoke calmly. "I am Ozymandias. I have fallen in love with your Miratrice, and she is equally taken with me. I am *not* your ancient enemy, and my adeptness at matching your powers lies in another source. Please believe me when I tell you this. I mean you no harm . . ."

Beldamo shook his head. "You don't understand. I could not believe you even if I wanted to. You have transgressed every natural law; you have broken every taboo. If you are a sorcerer, and I have seen nothing to refute that fact, then you must be a renegade of the lowest order. And there is only one renegade among us who would dare do as you have done—*Blaeus!*"

In speaking that final word, as though a battle oath, Beldamo flung himself across the chamber and crashed into Ozymandias.

Instantly he felt the wizard's hands reaching into his flesh, his fingers slipping around his enlarged organs, his blood vessels, and his heart. Within his skull, fingers, or something worse, wormed about his brain. The pressure began at once and Ozymandias remembered the cragar and how it had been killed. Inches from his face. Beldamo's eyes bored into him, and Ozymandias could see only the glimmer of death within the darkened pools. He remembered what it had been like to kill the creature, to snuff out its life and to momentarily feel an empathic rush of pain so exquisitely sharp and *real* as to leave an everlasting brand upon his mind. In a flash, as the pressure from Beldamo's grip threatened to burst his heart, to collapse the delicate layers of his brain.

Thoughts rushed through him, swirling in oily conflict, and he wrestled with the idea of killing the old man. This was no hunger-ravaged wolf, but a human being, a member of the species which Ozymandias had so longed to join. To kill Beldamo would be a negation of all that Ozymandias held sacred, and yet there was the defense of self-defense. Kill or be killed.

The alternatives rushed through him, and he used his psychokinetic touch to reach inside where the wizard's invisible hands were tightening upon his heart. Although there were no hands to touch, Ozymandias touched them, feeling the withered flesh, the bulging veins, the slender bones. He imagined them as much as felt them, but that did not matter. The important thing was that he could *feel* them, and from that point he could battle with the strength of Beldamo.

Fingers touched, grazed, curled. He grabbed the spidery hands of Beldamo and, as if unpeeling a crab from its rocky perch, pried away the fingers until the pressure on his heart was relieved. The power of the old man was surprisingly great, and the resolve to resist was that of a driven, obsessed man.

So convinced must Beldamo have been that he was battling his age-old adversary that he attacked Ozymandias with the fury forged in the ovens of memory and hate.

"Blaeus!" screamed the old man. "You bastard, I won't make the same mistake twice. You'll die at my hands this time, or I will die in the trying . . ."

The spoken words had weakened his psychic grip, and Ozymandias further pulled Beldamo away from his inner chest cavity. He thought that he detected the old man weakening slightly and experienced less difficulty holding the sorcerer at bay in a frozen, psychic standoff. Perhaps he could now use the pause to talk, to reason with the old man . . .

Before that could happen, however, the giant image of the wizard began to dwindle, instantly reminding Ozymandias that they had been grappling with one another's larger-than-life forms, part of the illusionary power of their apparently unconscious minds. Beldamo was presumably using the element of surprise to his advantage, and for an instant, as he returned to normal stature, slipped away from the psychic hold of Ozymandias.

The wizard hobbled quickly to the other end of the study as Ozymandias cast off his own illusion to give chase. There was a flash of light and, momentarily blinded, Ozymandias did not see the fusillade of energy bolts burst from the weaving fingers of Beldamo.

The bolts struck him with paralyzing effect, and he felt as though his chest and face had been pierced by white-hot lances. Falling upon his back, the thought passed through him that this was how it was going to end for him, and that he would face the mysterious moment called death with so little preparation that it did not even matter that his dying was at hand.

Something shadowy stood above him and the configuration of Beldamo shifted vaguely before his stunned eyes.

"Can it be so easy, enemy mine?" asked Beldamo. "You have lost the killing edge, and you shall pay with your life!"

Dazed, Ozymandias forced himself to speak. "I am not Blaeus . . . please . . . believe me."

Beldamo grinned sarcastically, then paused as a new thought touched him. For the first time, a hint of doubt colored his expression. "Another trick, perhaps," he said, raising his right hand above Ozymandias. "And yet, you may be truthful. I sensed that you could have bested me back then, back when you pulled my grip from your heart; you had me then, you could have turned things around and killed *me . . .*"

"But I did not."

"No," said Beldamo. "You did not. That is something Blaeus would have never done. Especially if he had traveled all that great distance to finish me. No, perhaps you tell the truth. It is possible that you are *not* Blaeus."

The respite in conversation had given Ozymandias the valuable time needed to recoup his strength. He felt his presence of mind returning, the cool rush of reason, and the tingling potentialities of psychic energy. If he chose he felt that he could flatten the old wizard with a bolt of psi power, gain the advantage, and maybe carry the battle once more.

But he waited.

There was indecision and careful thought in Beldamo's face. There was time for reason, if he wanted it so.

"My name is Ozymandias, not Blaeus. I am a student of the Ancient Arts, and I have fallen in love with Miratrice. That is the sum of things. I swear it."

"Perhaps you are correct," said Beldamo, not appearing to notice that Ozymandias had recovered from the stunning blows of his last attack. Shrugging, the old man raised his hand a bit higher. "At any rate, you still must die . . ."

"But why?" Ozymandias tensed for a counterattack.

Beldamo grinned and tilted his head philosophically. "Because you have violated my granddaughter, fool! She is bound by ancient law and must be given only to a Sorcerer of the Innermost Circle. She cannot marry one such as you!"

Again Beldamo raised his hand even a bit higher, preparing to administer the *coup de grâce*.

"Wait!" cried Ozymandias. "Beldamo, *think* about what you have just said! Think about it!"

"I *have* thought about it. I am correct, as usual. And so . . ."

"Yes, you *are* correct, but you have overlooked a very important thing: I *am* a worthy husband for Miratrice! Am I not qualified to be a Sorcerer of the Innermost Circle? Have I not held my own against the greatest of all wizards, the first Sorcerer of the Innermost Circle? Who else could do such a thing? Accepting of course that I am not Blaeus, and do not wish to kill you . . ."

Beldamo's right hand dropped perceptibly and new thoughts clouded his expression. His gray eyebrows thickened and knotted as he considered the logic of the questions. "Granted, you must *not* be Blaeus for what you say to make sense. And, further granted, you have displayed powers which only the greatest of wizards may possess, albeit you are still little more than a boy. Still further granted, you could be qualified to the Innermost Circle, despite the lack of family breeding . . . I could attest to your bloodline if I chose. There are none who would challenge my word . . ."

Beldamo paused and studied Ozymandias for a moment, then continued.

"You *do* love Miratrice? You are no base womanizer? Tell me true, now!"

"I am hardly that. My experience with women is scant, with love even less. But I have been told that one recognizes the reality when it touches him."

"Yes, you speak wisely, if not totally convincingly. I only wish that there were some way of proving to me that you are not Blaeus . . ."

"I can see that that possibility disturbs you greatly. Is there no way you might search my mind? I would submit to any proof you might require. What I tell you is true, Beldamo. I do swear it."

The old wizard's hand lowered further as he considered

the newest suggestion, and Ozymandias felt that he was probably going to survive the ordeal without further incident. Until that point, the question had been fairly moot.

"Yes, perhaps there is a way," said Beldamo. "Will you trust me to place you into a hypnogogic trance?"

"Your word that I will be safe is all that I would require."

Beldamo dropped his hand to the side of his gray musty robe. "I have almost achieved proof enough with that statement," he said grinning. "Blaeus would never trust me like that."

"Then perhaps it is not necess—" Ozymandias brightened and was cut off.

"But I will still put you under. Just to make sure, you understand." The old man winked and motioned that Ozymandias rise up from the floor.

"Yes, I understand. Shall we do it here? Now?"

"Why not?" Beldamo shrugged.

"Should we not look in on Miratrice? She might be worried about both of us. She might be—"

"She is a resourceful young woman. I have taught her well in most things. She will be all right." Beldamo waved off the conversation with a flip of his hand, pointing to a dais in the corner of the room. "Over there, lad. Lie upon it."

Ozymandias obeyed, crossing the room slowly, wondering what Kartaphilos might think if his friend knew what was to take place. There was no way of telling what the people of Gnarra's attitudes were concerning the First Age on a deep, unconscious level. The revelation of Ozymandias's true identity might prove to be worse than simply being the vengeful enemy Blaeus.

"Now, on your back, hands behind your head. I want you to stare at the highest point in the ceiling. Relax and open your mind to suggestion. No barriers. No resistance."

Beldamo stood over the dais as Ozymandias reclined. He spoke in soft, reassuring tones that seemed to surge with restrained power and authority.

"Before we begin, could you perhaps explain exactly what you will be doing?"

Beldamo regarded this question with a guarded, skeptical expression.

"I am *still* a student at heart," said Ozymandias quickly.

"Oh, yes, of course. I had almost forgotten. Very well. Once you are comfortably entranced, I shall enter your mind, much as a mourning dove might silently glide among the boughs of a thick forest. I shall move quickly throughout the branches of your mind, but will alight at no place. I shall not disturb even the smallest leaf, but I shall see everything. Your memories, your fears, your true feelings, will become known to me. If you are who you say you are, I shall know it. If there are any barriers erected against my flight, I shall detect them. If there is any conscious effort at dissembling or illusion, I shall detect it also. That is not a warning, merely a statement of fact."

Ozymandias nodded. "All right, Beldamo. Remember one thing: I trust you."

The sensations did not begin immediately, and for a moment he felt that the trance was not taking hold. He felt restless in the fashion of one who seeks to find a comfortable position in which to fall asleep, but is unable to do so. His mind seemed sharp and alert, and not at all in readiness to become entranced. It was only at that instant of seeming keenness that he heard a low susuration in his inner ears, a growing buzzing sound that suddenly filled his skull with its droning sound. It grew so loud that it became the only sound, the greatest, most overwhelmingly complete sound that he had ever heard. It was as though the droning sound were the only sound he had ever experienced and he felt a relentless desire to merge with the sound, to become one with the sound and be lost in its completeness. For an instant he felt the desire to move, to activate a muscle in his hand, his toes, his face, but there was no somatic response. It was a feeling of total paralysis, but not in the usual sense. It was not that his body was not receiving nervous commands to move, but rather that his mind refused to issue the commands in the first place. Momentary flashes of paranoia blanketed him. Betrayal. Death. Blackness. All loomed at a dark threshold beyond his meager, sound-filled perceptions. He could see nothing, and yet could see everything. It was as though he were conscious of the study, of Beldamo's presence, yet could not genuinely see or feel any of it. If Beldamo was indeed probing within his mind, he was not aware of it. There was no sensation of intrusion, of violation, of danger. Time had no meaning and there was no sense of passage—simply being, in the purest, simplest meaning of the term. There was a serene knowledge of merely existing, with no further pressures or obligations other than acceptance of that single fact. I am, thought Ozymandias, and it was all that mattered . . .

CHAPTER 8

"He knows everything," said Ozymandias, pacing slowly about the small dusty confines of their quarters.

"How could you allow such a thing?" asked Kartaphilos, obviously upset by the tale he had just heard.

"If I told you 'for love,' you would not be satisfied, would you?"

"Satisfied, no. Reminded of my humanity, yes." He chuckled and shook his head. "Oh, my friend, it is amazing how tightly we can weave the webs about ourselves, is it not?"

"I'm beginning to learn just how tightly, yes."

"And what was his reaction to what you have told him, or rather, what you allowed him to discover?"

"Well, he wants to meet you . . ."

"I'm not surprised. I mean, what are his more general feelings?"

"In light of his mind tapping, he could not deny what he had learned, and therefore he was forced to undergo what the Gnarrans call *hisei*, which is a calm, phenomenological acceptance of things as they simply *are*. It is an abandonment of emotional attachment or reaction to a truth or a discovery, so that its impact may be properly integrated into the perceiver's now altered world view."

"You mean that he did not get upset, excited, distressed, or any other typically human reaction?" Kartaphilos smiled as he listened to his friend's deft use of Gnarran philosophical jargon.

"Yes, exactly. Afterward, though, I did feel him out on his prior attitudes and feelings concerning the First Age, and was quite surprised to learn that the Sorcerers of the Isle are quite favorably predisposed to the First Age."

"Why so?"

"For several reasons, actually. You see, they believe that the World—not just this continent or this planet, but the Cosmos in general—is all quietly related and connected. Their writings speak of an inevitable progression, a cosmic evolution, which will pass through seven levels. What is known as the First Age, in terms of Gnarran cosmology, is actually the Third Level. Meaning that there were two previous ages, or levels, before that particular era, and that we are presently enduring the Fourth Level, which was long ago prophesied as low point in the cosmic evolutionary cycle—a time of restoration and rebirth, a time of darkness and ignorance, in which only a select few would be pressed to carry on the knowledge and the spiritual beliefs necessary for the advancement to next level. The Fourth Level of Existence is the pivotal point, the centerpiece, and the crucible in which the future histories of humankind must be forged."

"This all sounds quite plausible," said Kartaphilos. "It is not unlike many other long-standing religions and philosophies. Go on . . ."

Ozymandias nodded, continued pacing slowly as he spoke. "Well, Beldamo believes that the First Age, as it is commonly called, was a necessary step in the evolutionary process. In fact, it was during the earliest years of the First Age that the Ancient Arts of the Sorcerers were actually collected, codified, and given the organization which binds them still today. In that sense the First Age was the revered era for the Gnarrans. The technology of the age was also viewed as necessary, if only to bring about the required Armageddon. You see, everything has been going according to plan, according to Beldamo and his belief system."

"I think I see where you are leading this," said Kartaphilos, "so forgive me if I cut your little history lesson short. Just tell me: where do you fit into all this?"

Ozymandias smiled. "Ah, said the playwright, there's the rub, right?"

Kartaphilos nodded. "You could say that, yes."

"Well, it seems that the Gnarran view includes the usual messianic figure, the rebirth mythos which will provide the next level with the necessary impetus to progress on the *next* level, and so on . . . Do you follow me?"

"Oh, yes, unfortunately, I do."

"It seems as though their writings include long passages which describe the end of the Third Level, the breakdown of technology and the loss of knowledge, save for small isolated pockets of little individual importance. The belief stands that from the ashes of the Third Level—or First Age—will rise up a figure who will represent all that was good and necessary, all that personified the Third Level, but was able to incorporate the new, functional aspects of the Fourth Level. You see, contrary to popular World belief, the Gnarran view is not antiscience, nor antitechnological. Their view of technology in general is simply different; they see humankind's penchant for the mechanical to be part of a larger organic whole. They see technology as every bit as essential as the chemical, bodily processes which give us that strange sensation called life."

Kartaphilos leaned forward at the table, steepling his fingers as he considered his next words. "And this messianic figure—Beldamo naturally assumes that *you* are this figure?"

Ozymandias blushed slightly. "Well, no, not yet, anyway. He says that it is of course too early to tell since I am

so young. But he does admit to liking the possibility that the
Ancient Texts may be proved correct, and that he may be
the agent of that proof."

"That does not surprise me. But what of his plans now—
assuming, that is, that he has plans for you?"

"Not in the strictest sense. He has, of course, agreed to
my marriage with Miratrice, and—"

"Yes, I meant to bring that up. Now listen to me, my
friend, before you lunge at my throat. I understand your
deep and sincerely felt emotions concerning Miratrice, and
believe it or not, in my long-ago youth I was as much in
love as you are this moment. But I must ask this question:
Are you sure that a marriage is a wise course for you to
follow . . . at this early stage in your development?"

"I expected your doubts on this," said Ozymandias.
"And I can fully understand your point of view. You see
this whole thing as a lark, perhaps, driven on only by the
glandular pressures of my youth. It is not so simple, I assure you. I do not plan to have my marriage defer my explorations of the World, nor my overriding desire to experience as much as possible, and possibly even to in some
small way affect the World. There are a thousand mysteries
into which I have yet to enter, much less understand. There
is art and music, poetry, economics, sociology, and politics,
all of which must be tasted and tried, and even aspects of
this World which I have yet to even consider. But there is
something else which has entered the overview of my life—
something I cannot ignore."

"The dramatic pause, appropriately placed," said Kartaphilos. "All right, now what is that final thing?"

"Miratrice is pregnant. She will bear me a child within
eight months. I must remain here at least until that point.
Afterward, she will be kept busy caring for the child, and
I will be free to travel if I wish. Gnarra is rather centrally
located and I will be able to return from almost any point

in the known World whenever I choose. Once the child is
old enough, my family can join us wherever we are at the
time."

Kartaphilos nodded. "Yes, that does change matters a
bit, doesn't it? You are fast becoming a man, Ozymandias.
It suits you well, although I am not sure of how well it
influences our purposes."

Ozymandias smiled. "And that brings up the next question: just exactly what *are* our purposes?"

Kartaphilos chuckled lightly and shook his head. "How
true, my friend, how deliciously true . . ."

The seasons drifted past, and with the coming warmth
of spring, Miratrice gave birth to a son. She survived the
ordeal with a minimum of risks, having the combined
knowledge of Ozymandias's technology and her grandfather's Ancient Arts. The infant boy was named Bysshe, in
a moment of ironic whim, by Ozymandias. He was dark-
haired like his father, but possessed the penetrating
eyes of his mother, which seemed to dart about the nursery
with a self-controlled awareness that was absent in most in-
fants. Ozymandias hoped dearly that he was genetically
special, but only time would provide the answer to that
question.

Kartaphilos had been living in the Keep ever since the
marriage, and he shared with Ozymandias and Beldamo in
the pursuit of knowledge and the learning of the Ancient
Arts. It was a curious union, all three being combinations
of different ages, worlds, and dreams. More curious still
was that they all meshed easily and comfortably, learning
from each other, growing ever more wise.

Also during this time of rest and retreat from the main-
streams of the World, Kartaphilos made use of the period to
keep abreast of the World developments as best he could.
Each day he spent a few hours down in the village, wind-

ing his way through the marketplace, the docks, and the
taverns, where he might pick up a piece of news from some
foreign port or capital. As the days passed, he became a familiar figure in the village, and the natives as well as sailors
and merchantmen lost their initial aversion to speaking
with him. Whereas Gnarra was centrally located within the
Gulf of Aridard, it was not a major source of trade. Its various port cities were used primarily for stopovers during
gulfwide shipping cruises, hence the many taverns and inns
for the enjoyment of weary crews. Such men are notorious
gossips and rumormongers, and their presence served as
an excellent source of new developments in World affairs.
With any fortune at all, Kartaphilos could expect to pick
up news only a month or so after its actual occurrence.

And so, as the months passed, he learned some interesting tidbits, which might prove useful to him and Ozymandias once they resumed their travels. To the north, the
Shudrapur Dominion continued in its role as the bread-
basket of the World. Its farmers and other growers never
failed to produce season after season of the most prized
wines, fruits, and grains. Its politics, as always, remained in
a low-profile, quietly functioning position, and posed no
threat to the rest of the World, nor, more importantly, to itself. This was said, despite reports that some of the Shudra-
purian trade vessels had been attacked, looted, and sunk by
sea raiders under the flag of the Behistar Republic. East of
the Shudrapur, however, the news of recent outrages of the
Behistar was causing unrest within the Scorpinnian Empire,
that vast nation of spartan existence. It seems, so the merchant seamen said that the emperor, a fat, dilatory figurehead of a ruler, was becoming upset with the loss of trading ships to his ports of Mogun and Talthek. The Behistar
pirates were depleting his supplies of wine, women, and
song. And so, Kartaphilos learned, the emperor had been
doing a bit of sword rattling by sending out some new

proclamations to his oxlike populace: there would be army conscriptions, and the placement of armed troops on all ships dealing with the Scorpinnian Empire, and no quarter would be taken with anyone attempting to disrupt trade with the empire. Although the emperor was largely ignorant of the exigencies of the Interdict placed upon the Behistar Republic by the rest of the World (the last war had been lost by the Behistarians, and as a result they were closely policed by the militaries of the neighboring countries), he was advised by his chiefs of staff and chancellors to exhibit concern and a show of force. This early reaction to the breaking of the Interdict was being met ambivalently by the various other nations of the World. G'Rdellia was advising caution, and a closer watch on the Luten of Behistar, formerly supposed to be the weak son of the last bellicose ruler of the Republic. Odo, characteristically, was quite philosophical in its outlook on the Behistar problem, publicly announcing that if another war proved necessary to summarily flatten the warmongers, then so be it. Zend Avesta, the country neighboring the aggressors to the west, was *very* concerned with Behistar's deportment. History had shown that Zend Avesta had been the first country officially attacked during the last war. That worthy nation of scientists and tinkerers would dislike very much to see their recent advances in technology and manufacturing be devastated by another World conflict. Their own messengers, couriers, and diplomats were encouraging a quick retaliation against the Luten. It was quite clear that quotidian affairs of the World were soon to be thrown into a large mixing bowl if stern measures were not quickly adapted. It was indeed unfortunate that only the most dire circumstances could force men of different cultures to work together.

There were, quite naturally, the personal colorations, embellishments, and prejudices of Kartaphilos's sources, but even then the cyborg understood the general implications of the news he received. Although the Isle of Gnarra would remain effectively neutral and consequently untouched by the coming war storm, Kartaphilos realized that the lives of he and Ozymandias might be greatly affected by it.

Also at this time, there were quiet developments taking place within the upper levels of Gnarra society and the Council of Five. Excited and surprised by the reports of Beldamo concerning the appearance of Ozymandias and his seemingly apt qualifications for insertion into the ancient writings, the Five Elders were preparing the way for the rise of Ozymandias to the status of a public figure, subgenre demagogue.

Kartaphilos was greatly disturbed by this turn of events, fearing that Ozymandias would become a political pawn in the hands of the council, which would use him to urge the populace to support whatever causes might be associated with the messianic character. It was not a good idea to place oneself so firmly in the public eye, even though Gnarra and its inner affairs were largely ignored by the rest of the World.

Kartaphilos met with resistance when he expressed his fears to Ozymandias. They were walking the parapets of the Beldamo's Keep, looking down upon the village just before sunset when Ozymandias brought up the future plans of the council.

"They want to induct into the Innermost Circle in a public ceremony," he was saying, not so much for the approval of Kartaphilos, but rather out of courtesy.

"I still say it's a risky business."

"Meaning I should not do it?"

"Exactly."

"But why? You and I both know that all this magic and

necromancy is foolishness. These people are merely advanced genetic mutants—scientists of the psi field. It has been a valuable place for me to develop the latent skill you yourself implanted in my own genes. How can you suddenly be against this?"

"Suddenly is an imprecise word. I have been studying the effects of this whole affair, Ozymandias, and I do not like the pattern which is emerging."

"How do you mean?" The young man stopped, leaned against the ramparts, staring at his old companion.

"Already, in the village below, the people are talking about you: small legends have quickly spread of your contest with Beldamo, with the victory you have won. In every corner, I hear snatches of conversations about dawning of the new age, the Next Level, brought about by your appearance on the scene. Talk about self-fulfilling prophecy —these people have a corner on the market."

"Surely it's not that bad." Ozymandias smiled.

"No, it's probably worse. Already you are losing your perspective. Think about what you are becoming! Knowledge unbounded, stretching back over millennia, available in total recall, tapping into the foremost sources in the history of civilization. Physical strength, endurance, and perfect health. Psi talents far more developed than those of anyone else in the World. And what are you doing with it all? Playing tin god to an island full of inbred congenitally defective mystics! Don't you see that they are just using you?"

"*Using* me? Of course not. They are only following the tenets of their culture. It is a natural thing, you know."

"Yes, perhaps it is. But my question is this: Why are *you* so comfortable in this role they are quietly assembling for you? Have you forgotten our past conversations about things like this? Don't you recall the lessons of prior ages?

Zarathustra? Odd John? Christ? Or is it that you *like* this mold you are being forced into? Do you think that you might be able to do a better job than your predecessors?"

Ozymandias smiled. "An interesting way of putting it, my old friend. I admit to having been thinking about these things, and I'm not at all sure what *is* actually happening to me, being planned for me. And that is precisely *why* I am playing it out. I want to *know* what will indeed happen."

"And in your knowledge, you might sow the seeds of your undoing." Kartaphilos turned away and took several steps farther down the battlement, stopped and regarded him dramatically.

Ozymandias looked at him as if not knowing what next to say.

"Listen, my young and curious friend. I am not *against* you, please believe me. Nor am I playing devil's advocate. It is simply that I worry about you, and feel responsible for you. You are my friend, my brother, and my son. You are the only thing that gives my life meaning, and you must understand that, and know why I express meddling concern."

Ozymandias paused and looked at his first and closest friend, remembering how important the relationship between them had become. Outwardly, the cyborg resembled a very old man. His long hair was gray and thick, his beard pepper-and-salt, and failing to hide the wrinkled, weathered face of an age-old wanderer. His eyes were sunk deeply into his steel skull etched with lines of age and wisdom. Synthetic though his flesh and body parts might have been, the bioneers who long ago constructed him had been gifted enough to provide him with a totally human aspect, so much so that his expressions of emotion were perfectly readable and transparent beneath the artificial flesh. Recently, Ozymandias had been training himself to be more sensitive to the empathic-telepathic emanations that all humans projected, and at that moment the feelings and thought impressions coming from Kartaphilos were strong and filled with the glow of sincerity.

As for his own feelings, Ozymandias felt ambivalent. By this time, he had become spiritually close to Miratrice and Beldamo, and their attendant culture of rich traditions; he had also begun to realize his indebtedness to Kartaphilos, who was indeed his father, brother, and friend. Every attempt to examine his own feelings, and perhaps more importantly, his motivations for what he now planned to do were met with curious blind spots—places in his consciousness which he seemingly could not fully view and understand. He was becoming hesitant to look at himself objectively, and he knew that this was more of that strange process of becoming human.

"Are you listening to me?" asked Kartaphilos, becoming disturbed by his friend's faraway look, his meditative silence.

"Yes, I'm sorry. I was listening only too well. I was thinking about what you've said . . ."

"And you have come to what conclusions?"

"That you are probably correct, but that I, in my impetuous youth, must find out for myself what is the best choice for me. I don't want to sound irreverent, so please forgive me if I seem so."

Kartaphilos shrugged. "No irreverence taken. How can I fault you for following the path of millions before you? It is most common for all men to let the words of experience fall deaf on them. There seems to be something inside us all which forces us to learn our mistakes only after we have committed them."

"And you are convinced that I am making a grave error?"

Kartaphilos nodded, but said nothing.

"Perhaps I should discuss the ceremony with Beldamo?"

"And tell him that *I* am sowing the seeds of doubt and fear within you? That would be yet another mistake."

"Surely you don't fear Beldamo—"

"Fear is not the correct word, no. I am not comfortable thinking that I would be viewed as a divisive factor in the future history of the Gnarran culture. And I dislike making unnecessary enemies."

"Then what should I do?" Ozymandias looked at him squarely, trying to communicate the feelings of pressure and the sense of desperation that was growing in him.

Kartaphilos smiled easily. "Please, my friend. You must do what you must do. Remember that you can never do anything in life that will please everyone. And also that in the final analysis, the most important person who must be pleased is *yourself*."

Neither man spoke for a moment as they both turned and absently looked down at the village and the gulf waters beyond. Kartaphilos was anxious to be through with the quasi-religious phase of Ozymandias's education; he wished to be on the road again. Ozymandias, on the other hand, was searching for his spiritual identity, and hoped that he would find it within the Gnarran view of existence.

In either case, both men looked forward to the following day when Ozymandias would be accepted into the Innermost Circle.

CHAPTER 9

In the center of the village of Hern lies the public square, in this case shaped like a pentagon, and called the Quara by the people. Its analogues throughout history were called the plaza, the agora, the marketplace, the forum, and the town hall. In Hern, the Quara is a meticulously laid out five-sided arena, sliced five ways by avenues which intersect at the center. The stones which delineate the Quara were inlaid with millennias-old mosaic tiles which reflect the sunlight with the intensity of fire opals. The tiles had been worn smooth and seamless under centuries of human traffic, but had retained their beauty and strength. The Quara was the focal point, the nexus, of all public affairs in all Gnarran cities and villages. It was the beginning point of festivals, weddings, funerals, executions, and official ceremonies.

It was here that Ozymandias stood upon a raised platform in concert with the Council of Five, the revered members of the Innermost Circle, and a sponsor, Beldamo. Off to the side of the central platform sat Miratrice and Kartaphilos; beyond them sprawled the five-sectioned tiers of the populace, all murmuring with the news that an outsider—a *nouri,* in the Gnarran tongue—was being initiated into the most sacred of necromantic hierarchies. Such a thing was unheard of in the history of the isle, and everyone deserted his or her job and duties to witness what would surely be a historic moment in the annals of Gnarran civilization.

The preparatory speeches and rituals were enacted with precision, pomp, and even a bit of circumstance as the Council of Five sat upon a raised platform in witness to it all. Immediately below the Five, on a special semidais, sat Ozymandias in the traditional gray robes of the Sorcerer. One of the members of the Innermost Circle approached him with a gold chalice, offering it to him slowly and with a certain amount of panache. He accepted the chalice and carefully drank its contents. At this point Beldamo rose and addressed the crowd, filling in the recent history of his acquaintance and subsequent sessions with his young apprentice. There were several sentences describing the young man's ability and perceptiveness, and his striking knack for learning even the most taxing of the Ancient Secrets. It was, to the ears of Kartaphilos, an uninspired introduction that flirted with platitude. Nevertheless, it appeared to please the crowd, and they began to murmur with the sweetness of anticipation as Beldamo gestured for Ozymandias to come forth and face the council.

For Ozymandias, he could not honestly admit to himself that he was enjoying the sum of the ritual and crowd-pleasing bag of tricks which the council had attached to the public ceremony. He found such proceedings to be exactly what they were: much flash and noise, but having little of substance or originality of expression. After having returned the ceremonial chalice to its bearer, he remained sitting, only half listening to the introduction of his former mentor and temporary adversary. As he sat, thinking of Miratrice and the feelings toward her, his son, and even Kartaphilos, he began to have twinges of regret at having agreed to the public spectacle. There was a sixth sense working within his mind at that moment, a kind of early-warning system which still only functioned at the subconscious level. There was a vague impression of something going wrong, but Ozymandias was not able to articulate what it actually might be. He felt a growing sensation of uneasiness—

—which gradually surrendered itself and its tension to a feeling of peacefulness. Something was happening to his sense of awareness and his ability to thoroughly control his thoughts, to keep them in concert with his perceptions and feelings. There came a vague suggestion that there was some kind of chemical response taking place within his body, and he could feel the process happening although he felt powerless to affect it. His training had provided him with a keen somatic awareness, over which he was learning to control even the most autonomic of body functions, but now he realized that essence of control was beyond him. A single clear thought pierced the mistiness which was fogging his mental centers. Less than conscious thought now, it became the image of the chalice and the dark, winelike liquid which had been contained within. He knew that the liquid had contained some kind of psychoactive drug, or perhaps an ancient herbal concoction. He knew now that he had been drugged for the purposes of the ceremony, but knew also that he was without the power to countermand whatever effects of the drug might be forthcoming.

There was a fading part of his awareness which told him that he should be alarmed, even enraged by this knowledge, but he could not muster the psychic energy to suitably react to the subterfuge. No, there were more attractive, more appealing stimuli which were taking precedence . . . A warm glow seemed to be surrounding his body, and he interpreted it as an outward manifestation of his strength and his special panoply of talents. Sitting, waiting for his name to be called, he held out his palms and looked at them carefully, and saw a bright-blue neon aura emanating from his flesh. Several cees thick the aura pulsed and throbbed in synchrony with the basic rhythms of his metabolism. Ozymandias began concentrating on the rhythmic pulses and became enraptured with the counterpoint of his own biofeedback. It was a mesmerizing, narcotic effect, which, compounded by the effects of the psychoactive drug, further removed him from the state of normal sensation.

His somatic sense betrayed him as he enjoyed an almost weightless feeling, which combined with the sensation of immense power. His body began to swell, to grow, and he felt himself growing larger, as if inflated like a balloon. The effect was so overwhelming that he was convinced that he was actually growing to gargantuan proportions. It was unlike his psychoinduced telekinetic sense, as experienced while battling Beldamo; no, this was an *inner,* somatic sensation, in which his brain centers were convinced that he was growing. There was a moment of panic, when he thought of how the crowd would react to the sudden appearance of such a giant in their midst, but it passed quickly when another part of his awareness took note that the crowd was *not* reacting adversely. Apparently the sudden increase in size was a part of the ceremony and the general populace had been expecting it. In that moment, he cast a casual glance about the crowd, up to the Council of Five, and even to his sponsor, wife, and friend. Smiling to them, he noticed that everyone else possessed a bright-blue aura about his or her bodies like himself, the only differences being slight variations in hue and intensity.

Cutting through the mist like the strong light of a beacon, Ozymandias heard his name being called.

There came a bright outburst of applause and approval from the crowd, and he could feel the eyes of everyone upon him. Beldamo gestured to him as he sat, wrapped in a swirling montage of hallucination. Ozymandias stood and faced the crowd, evoking another burst of applause, and raised his hands in a show of greeting. As he did so, he became fascinated with the stroboscopic trails of his hands as they arched upward, leaving a path of semivisible images. For an instant the crowd and the ceremony were forgotten as he concentrated upon the fantastic perceptions which now flooded into him. He flicked his hand through the air in a long, graceful arc and watched a stream of sparkling matter issue forth from his palm to leave a path which glittered like a comet's tail. Again, he waved his arm, and watched the sparkling trails describe the arc of his hand. Pausing he examined his palm closely and was amazed to see miniature suns and planets streaming forth from his flesh as if by magic. The effect was at once hypnotic and ecstatic; it was as though he were caught within the throes of creation itself, and he found the experience totally intoxicating.

His name was again called, and he was jerked from his personal visions by the outer reality of the crowd and the ceremony to come.

Answering Beldamo, he followed the next request to come forward and slowly, weightlessly, approached the raised platform where the Council of Five awaited him. They spoke slowly and with much solemnity as he stood facing them, but their words were distorted, as if stretched out, and pronounced so weightily that he could not understand them. Ozymandias did not care. So enraptured by the drug state he experienced that he was not concerned with mere words. Occasionally, recognizable terms penetrated his altered state of being.

Millennia.

Prophecies.

Signs and portents.

He comprehended the words, but there was a part of him

which refused to attach any significance to them. It was simply much easier, and far preferable, to flow with the exquisite joy of the altered instant.

Someone called his name again, and he was distracted from the business of creating new worlds with the sweep of a hand . . .

The weather was uncommonly warm, and Kartaphilos could see that many of the members of the crowd were perspiring and squirming on their benches to be comfortable. He was thankful, as he often was, for not being burdened with a body of flesh and blood. Marvelous biological mechanism that it was, the human body was far inferior to the duralloy body of the cyborg. Self-repairing, fusion-powered, the body would last indefinitely and was, of course, impervious to such minor things as changes in the weather, as well as more formidable dangers.

The ceremony of the Innermost Circle was growing long and tedious, and there had not been much mention or acknowledgment of Ozymandias until he had been offered the chalice of ceremonial wine. The major thought of Kartaphilos would be that the entire display would soon be at an end. He had little patience for carefully constructed public displays which were intended only for the enjoyment of the masses and had very little value or substance once you removed the flash and the glitter. It was unfortunate that the World had slipped so badly after the last great war, and was only now groveling back from a new Dark Age of Ignorance, Fear, and Superstition.

His thoughts continued to wander and drift, paying little attention to the speeches and minor rituals that were being offered to the crowd. It was only when they called Ozymandias's name and Beldamo introduced him with a small, prosaic preamble that Kartaphilos began to take serious notice. Miratrice sat by his side, cradling the young Bysshe close to her breasts and admiring her young husband with all due pride. Kartaphilos wished that he could share her good wishes and warm feelings, but he could not escape the feeling that the public ceremony would not be beneficial in the long run.

Looking up, he saw that Ozymandias had stood up to face the crowd while they applauded like proper groundlings. He saw immediately that there was something wrong. Ozymandias's features appeared to be slightly altered; there was something different about his entire aspect. The way he stood, the tilt of his head, the odd, semidazed expression of his face. His usually bright blue eyes were glassy and fixed; his mouth, always expressive and sharp, was now slack and half-open.

They have drugged him, thought Kartaphilos, and he does not realize it. Anger flared within him for an instant as he thought to rush the stage and carry off his poor dazed friend, to call an end to this charade which had been silly but was now assuming a more monstrous aspect. Stiffening visibly, Kartaphilos attempted to regain self-control, to let his more rational side examine the alternatives to rash violence.

Leaning close to Miratrice, he whispered: "Do they always drug the Initiates?"

The expression on her young face telegraphed her reply. "Why, no, of course not! Why do you ask?"

"Look at your husband closely. Does he not appear odd to you?"

After a moment's pause for inspection she answered in a soft voice. "I'm not sure. His eyes . . . they *do* look strange . . ."

"What's he doing now?" asked Kartaphilos as he pointed to his friend, who was now staring at his hands, then waving them about in grandiose gestures, seemingly oblivious to the crowd.

"I don't know," said Miratrice, and Kartaphilos noticed the beginning traces of panic in her voice.

"The bastards," muttered Kartaphilos, feeling a sense of helplessness wash over him as he studied the situation more closely. He was too far away from the podium to attempt to successfully rush it, and there were far too many underlings, bodyguards, and simple crowd members to allow for the rush of a single man. There was nothing he could do but watch . . .

And it proved to be quite a spectacle.

After a short display of fascination with his hands, there followed some strutting about the stage, as though Ozymandias was totally consumed by some private vision, enacting a part in some personal fantasy. Kartaphilos found it to be degrading and more than humiliating. The young sorcerer-to-be was then addressed by the Council of Five in a language which was unrecognizable to the cyborg, and he assumed that it was the original tongue of the Ancient Gnarrans of the First Age. He assumed that Ozymandias could understand the language by dint of his studies with Beldamo.

After being addressed by the council, Ozymandias turned and faced the crowd, whereupon a great cheer rose up from them. Spreading his arms, Ozymandias posed for them, in the posture of a great leader, a hero, a demagogue . . . and Kartaphilos shuddered as he considered the aptness of that last descriptive word . . .

Then Ozymandias lowered his left hand, pointing his right straight up to the heavens. High above the assembly drifted several white-tufted clouds, having neither the density nor the size to obscure the unseasonably hot sun. Pointing to the nimbus formation, Ozymandias arched his back. There was a large collective gasp from the crowd as a bright-blue bolt of light emanated from his hand, lancing upward to pierce the clouds. In an instant, the cloud grew dark and heavy, roiling with internal pressures of temperature gradients. Increasing in size, the formation swelled to eventually blot out the sun, leaving the assembly in a well of subdued, shadowy light. For another moment the crowd was silent, obviously stunned by the power of the young sorcerer.

Kartaphilos himself was shocked by the display, for in the purest visual sense it was very impressive, and something that usually could only be found in the fanciful descriptions of various religious texts, which sought to prove the power and glory of whatever lionized figure was being depicted. What made the display even more impressive to Kartaphilos was his personal knowledge that the act had not been the product of illusion or mass hypnosis. Being equipped with artificial eyes, which covered the entire part of the visible spectrum and some shadings into the red and violet areas, Kartaphilos's visual proprioceptors would not have been deceived by a mere illusion or visual trick. This could only mean that Ozymandias had learned how to use his psychokinetic powers to actually exert immense influence over physical objects.

There was a dramatic pause upon the raised platform as Ozymandias retained his thunderbolt-hurling stance. The Council of Five loomed above him, expressionless, but obviously approving of his pyrotechnics. The crowd hanging on the edge of tension awaiting his next move. It came with unexpected suddenness as he raised his left arm, again pointing to the sky, and releasing another bolt of bright-blue light, which jumped up to the dark clouds in an eyeflash. There followed a thunderous crash, and a yellow-white explosion which instantly disintegrated the cloud.

The shadows were dispersed by the brilliant flash and the Quara was again washed in the warm sunlight. The sky was now cloudless and stained with a dark, moody blue that was characteristic of the isle's season.

Again there was a roar of approval from the crowd and Ozymandias this time acknowledged their presence by bowing deeply, ending with a flourish of his right hand. As he straightened to face them again, he outstretched his hands and closed his eyes. Within moments an orange-yellow aura began to dance about the edges of his body, completely haloing him in an outline of lightly dancing fire. There came a rumble of awe from the crowd, with the screams of several more emotional types who at first thought that their hero had been set mysteriously aflame. When Ozymandias did not seem to react adversely to the aura of fire, the screams subsided and deadly calm enveloped the crowd.

Kartaphilos shook his head as he watched the display, as if the gesture might dispel the spectacle. It was simultaneously horrifying and exciting, and even Kartaphilos felt in conflict with his emotions as he witnessed the bizarre event. The aura of fire continued to corruscate about his body. Ozymandias remained rigid and cruciform as he began to rise from the platform. Again the crowd gasped collectively as they watched the levitation begin.

High into the air his body rose, slowly, majestically. The crowd was now blanketed by shocked silence, each member's gaze firmly fixed on Ozymandias. He continued to ascend until he was so distant that his features were indistinct, so that he resembled a burning cross high in the air.

Kartaphilos craned back to see his companion, instantly reminded of Constantine. *In hoc signo vinco,* he thought, and wondered if the Council of Five, or even Beldamo,

were familiar with the medieval myths of the First Age. If
so, this entire display might be a foreshadowing of further
manipulations, of greater machinations in a Worldwide
scheme. Shaking his head, he looked about the crowd, and
could not avoid seeing the expressions of awe, blended
nicely with acceptable amounts of old-time religious adula-
tion. *The making of a messianic figure,* he thought cyni-
cally.

Miratrice was tugging at the sleeve of his robe, breaking
his flow of concentration. Speechless, she could only point
upward. As Kartaphilos looked up, he saw that the aura of
light had intensified about Ozymandias, resembling a solar
corona effect, which caused the crowd to issue forth low
murmurings of fear and surprise.

Like a gathering fireball, the light and the energy seemed
to collect about his body, building up a charge, until there
was a great explosive *crack,* following a beam of blue-
white light, passing from Ozymandias to a volcanic peak
beyond the inland valley. In a blinding flash the tip of the
mountain disintegrated, followed by a rolling clap of
thunder and crumbling debris; the sounds echoed across
the valley, shocking the crowd into fearful silence. Now the
aura about his body became more subdued, and slowly, almost without notice, he began to descend.

As though there had been a signal to the crowd, their
silence was broken with murmurings like those of small
creatures who huddle in the bushes afraid to approach a
camper's fire. Behind Kartaphilos, he could hear phrases
from some of the closer members of the crowd. He heard
specific words, spoken in awe that was reserved for only
the most sacred of things. Kartaphilos was familiar with
the words. The history of man was littered with the broken
fragments such words eventually caused.

Looking up to the platform, he saw Ozymandias reach

the base of the platform. He stood for a moment, arms extended in a symbol of triumph, then collapsed into the arms of two waiting attendants.

If this was a new beginning, thought Kartaphilos, it was a bad omen indeed.

CHAPTER 10

It was more than two days before Kartaphilos, before anyone save Miratrice, was allowed to see him. It was said that
Ozymandias had fallen into a deep sleep, perhaps even a
coma, after the spectacular display of his powers, and that
only the combined magicks of Beldamo and the other
members of the Innermost Circle had been able to save
him from death. Kartaphilos, upon hearing this, had
checked the local library editions of the Ancient Texts,
under the headings of prophecies, levels, and messiahs.

He was not surprised to see that everything was progress-
ing according to the "divine" word.

"They drugged you," he said, as he entered the room
where Ozymandias lay on a large fluffy bed. The shutters
had been drawn and little light filtered through the thick
slats.

"That is a fine greeting." Ozymandias attempted to
smile, but managed only a poor facsimile.

"It is true, is it not?" Kartaphilos walked to the window
and threw open the shutters, filling the room with afternoon light.

"Yes, it is true. But I did not know, I swear to you."

"I believe you. That is not important now. The damage
has been done. And we must talk, my friend." Kartaphilos
turned and stared at his friend. There was a serious expression on his face that could not have been employed by his
machine parts.

"I was expecting this, and I hate to admit it, but I agree with you. We must talk."

Sitting down at the foot of the bed, Kartaphilos nodded, looked away, past the windows, as though attempting to properly phrase what he would say next. "I don't want to start by saying 'I told you so,' but it seems like the only appropriate opening."

"I agree. Go on, what is your plan? You must have a plan."

Kartaphilos smiled. "I always do, don't I? Yes, well, this is no exception. My plan is quite simple, however. We escape from here as soon as possible."

"Do you think escape is the right word? And what about Miratrice? And Bysshe?"

"Escape is definitely the right word. The Gnarran constabulary has placed a special cadre of their finest all about the entrances to Beldamo's Keep. The Promontory Road now has a guard booth, and all common citizens must receive passes to come to and from this place. That includes regular deliveries and services. If we are to leave this place, we will most positively be effecting an escape."

"And you feel this is because of the Council of Five?"

Kartaphilos chuckled. "It is certainly not the work of Howdy Doody."

"Who? Oh, yes, that First Age entertainer, correct?"

"After a fashion, yes. Now listen to me . . . Like many religious factions of past eras, the council has been growing impatient with their kit bag of prophecies. They are wise men, and wise men realize that the populace can be placated and controlled by pie-in-the-sky claptrap for only a short time. Years or centuries, depending on how enlightened your populace might be. At any rate, the length of time is immaterial. Despite the party line that the Gnarrans are indifferent to the political ebbs and flows of the rest of

the World, I believe they are very much interested in how
their brothers and sisters about the Aridard are getting
along."

"Why?"

"Because I have been getting reports from the merchant
sailors that the Behistar Republic is breaking the rules of
the Interdict. Some believe that there is going to be another
war very soon."

"How soon?"

"That is hard to tell. Communications among the nations
are erratic at best, slow in the usual. Mobilization and concert are unknown elements at the moment. There is no way
to know when the war will begin, but it seems inevitable
nonetheless."

"But what does this have to do with the Gnarrans?"

Kartaphilos looked at him. "I think you should be able
to figure this one out. You are growing wiser by the day—
at least I *hope* that you are. Use that memory of yours.
Pull out some facts, some correlations; see what you come
up with."

Ozymandias nodded, feeling somewhat embarrassed.
"All right, let's see . . . If we assume that the Gnarrans are
interested in the World political situation, then we must
also assume that they wish to exert some kind of influence
over the rest of the World."

"Quite so."

"Let's try this, then. The council sees the World finally
digging out of the ruins, that within the next century or so,
there might be some *real* stable civilizations in the making.
The ascension to the next level, as they would say . . . and
perhaps they now wish to have some kind of power in the
World."

"That's right, go on . . ."

"All right, assuming that they want power, it seems logical to say that they will want to shape the 'new' World to their own view of the cosmos. The question is, how do they expect to gain power?"

"Precisely," said Kartaphilos. "Any ideas on that?"

"Only the most obvious, the most time-worn winner."

"Which is?"

Ozymandias shrugged. "A holy war. A crusade. A *jihad*. Call it whatever you want, it's still the same thing."

"My feelings exactly. You see, you had all the answers all the time."

"You really believe that the council wishes to bring about some kind of Worldwide war, in the name of their religion? With *me* as their rallying point?"

Kartaphilos nodded "Undoubtedly with you as their point of focus, their seat of power. Believe me, my friend, that display the other day has still got the people mumbling. Word has by now spread throughout the isle and is making its way to the mainland. I wouldn't be surprised if the government in Eleusynnia has already made the connection. If not, they will, and other nations will not be far behind."

"What does this all mean? In terms of me, I mean. In terms of all of us?"

"It depends on what we do, don't you think? If we stay here and let you become a pawn, a figurehead for the masses, you may become a reluctant military leader. Hundreds of thousands could be slaughtered in your name."

Ozymandias shook his head.

"You *know* it could happen," said Kartaphilos, continuing.

Ozymandias nodded quickly. "Then we must get out of here. Now."

"That's what I've been telling you. Are you feeling strong enough for a long journey?"

"How long?"

"I'm not sure. I think we should book passage on a ship heading southwest. Perhaps the best place to be right now would be Zend Avesta. They are the most level-headed people on the gulf, for my money. They are the least likely to be influenced by the rumors of a superman that will be flying about pretty soon. I have made plenty of acquaintances down by the docks, and our supply of Odonian silver has never failed to motivate men of lesser means."

"There are other problems, you know . . ."

Kartaphilos nodded. "I know. Miratrice and the boy. I've already considered all that. We can't leave them here, or the council might use them as leverage to get you to return."

"You think they would actually threaten them, even hurt them?"

Kartaphilos chuckled. "Desperate men will do many terrible things. Our problem is that we do not know how desperate the council might be. And I have no wish to find out. My feeling is that we take Miratrice and the child with us, then deposit them in a monastery or a convent somewhere in eastern Avesta. They would be safe there, I assure you."

"Are you positive? How do you know this?"

"I have used the monasteries for centuries. The abbots are most agreeable to intelligent visitors, especially if they have heavy pockets. I have never met a man of the cloth who did not appreciate fine wine, fine art, and the other things that silver may provide."

"All right, I'll trust you even in this. Now, when do we leave? And how do we get past these guards you spoke of?"

"First a few questions. Of the powers you displayed the other day, how much control do you have over them? Do you feel confident in them, or do you think that they were more the effect of the drugs? If you are as potent as you seemed, we will have little trouble getting out of here."

"I'm not exactly sure how much control I have. The hallucinations seemed to prompt a lot of what I was doing. The levitation is something I had been training for with Beldamo, and I have some degree of control over it. I believe that I will eventually be able to move while levitating, actually fly through the air."

Kartaphilos nodded appreciatively. "What about that energy you used to explode the mountaintop?"

"Your guess is as good as mine. To paraphrase others before me, I didn't know I had it in me. I don't know what it is other than a gathering of psychic energies and focusing them very tightly toward a particular object. Until I try it again, I don't know if I can do it or not. I know what you're thinking, though. Just send a blast at the guards and that would be that, right?"

"Of course."

"There's a problem with that, you know."

"Your ethical nature, no doubt?"

Ozymandias nodded.

"I'm sorry, my friend, but you must remember that I was originally a warrior. The elimination of lives was my profession."

"I know that. It's just that I'm not sure I can imagine myself doing it."

Kartaphilos smiled. "You are not the first man to feel this way. If it comes down to another life or your own, feelings have a way of changing."

"Self-preservation? Ah, yes, the 'we are all animals' view."

"You have the luxury of being able to smirk—for now."

Ozymandias looked away for a moment, trying to justify what Kartaphilos had proposed. Perhaps his friend was correct and that a totally philosophical approach to life was unrealistic. The pragmatists of history had always seemed to be the most successful; the ones who had not denied their origins, their heritage of the caves.

Turning back to his friend, he asked him if Miratrice had been told of the plan.

"No, I felt that would be too presumptuous of me. I know that you will want to tell her."

"You were correct. I'll tell her as soon as we're ready. What about our supplies? The 'crawler?"

"I have already arranged for some of the stevedores who drink regularly at the Broken Gull to load it upon the *Hidden Dream,* a frigate bound for Zend Avesta. They think it's a museum piece to be placed in the Hall of Technology at Borat. The ship leaves, appropriately enough, at dawn. I also have booked passage for four in its cabins. Not a luxury cruise, but it will do nicely."

"So we must leave sometime tonight."

"Yes, but I would prefer to be able to time it as closely as possible to the *Dream*'s departure. I don't want too much time elapsing with us hanging around just waiting to be discovered. I think there will be plenty of confusion surrounding our escape, and if we can board ship and be off while the chaos still reigns, we have a better chance of avoiding detection."

"What about the ship's captain? Does he know he's kidnapping the nation's most popular sorcerer?"

"Doesn't know, and wouldn't give a damn anyway. I've spent many an hour matching flagons of ale with him. He's a practical, no-nonsense sailor, who believes in his compass and little else. He isn't interested in local politics or religion."

"Sounds like a smart man."

"Not really. Common sense is not the same as intelligence. But that is not important, is it? After dinner, I will attempt to visit again. I don't know if they are allowing you many visitors, since the official word is that you are re-cuperating from your 'religious' experience. Use the time between now and nightfall to explain everything to Mira-trice."

"That's going to be difficult."

"I thought you said that she understood you? That you had told her all about yourself, about me, about every-thing?"

Ozymandias nodded. "Yes, that is correct. I did. But you have to remember that she has never been away from her home. Never left the isle. To tell her that she must leave and possibly never come back is going to be difficult for her to accept."

"Yet you must tell her, and she must come with us."

"Suppose she refuses?"

Kartaphilos looked squarely into his eyes. "She will not refuse. If we must, we will subdue her with drugs or hyp-nosis. Ozymandias, you cannot leave her here. You know that."

"I know you are correct."

"Then we shall leave an hour before dawn. I will come for you then."

"What about the guards outside this corridor?"

Kartaphilos shrugged. "I don't think they will present any serious difficulties. Now, listen, here is the route of es-cape I have worked out. Review it with me and tell me your thoughts . . ."

The plan had been well thought out, and there were no glitches which Ozymandias could see. After a silencing of the interior guards, they would make their way to the lower catacombs of the Keep, where Beldamo had provided a tunnel beneath the battlements to a seldom used, little known trail and staircase that had been cut directly into the face of the cliff beneath the overhang of the Keep itself. All the ancient castles of Gnarran cliffs were so equipped that the ancient lords and kings would have an easy escape route in the event of a successful attack against their ramparts. The advantage of using the staircase was that it lay hidden from the view of anyone standing watch along the battlements. If no alarm were sounded, they would be able to descend the entire face of the promontory without being seen. Once into the village below, it was a short trip through the back streets to the docks and the waiting vessel.

This was how Ozymandias explained the escape to Miratrice, who reacted with expected shock and disbelief. She passed through various emotional states from surprise to anger to fearful hysteria, ending only when he told her that Kartaphilos was prepared to drug her if necessary to see that she complied with the plan. After that, his young wife sank into a state of depressed resignation, and refused to speak with him any more on the subject. At first, Ozymandias suspected that she might attempt to warn her grandfather of the escape, and he almost told her that she would have to remain with him until the time of departure.

Looking at her as she sat upon his bed, dressed in an evening robe, her face warmed and accented by ensconced torchlight, she resembled nothing more than a trembling bird who sensed it was trapped and had no defenses left. She was a beautiful woman, and he loved her deeply. He felt that if he displayed the distrust which flirted in his mind, something basic and necessary to their relationship would be destroyed. He knew that Kartaphilos would have advised taking no chances, and would have insisted on detaining Miratrice, but Ozymandias felt incapable of doing such a thing.

They simply stared at one another for a time before he spoke again.

"Will you come with us then? Without intervention from Kartaphilos?"

"That half-man of yours?" she said softly, satirically. "He's not even *half* a man, is he? What does he know about feelings?"

"You are not answering my question," he said.

Looking away, fighting the urge to cry once again, Miratrice drew her breath deeply. "Yes, I will go with you. You are my husband, and I have no choice."

"And you love me," he added.

"Yes, and I love you."

"You must try to understand why we must do this. Kartaphilos does not trust your grandfather's motives, and neither do I. Whether or not you are aware of it, there *is* a war brewing, and I told you I don't want people killed in *my* name. Didn't you understand what I was saying?"

Miratrice could only nod her head, still unable to look at him.

"Miratrice, please believe me . . . I would stay here if I thought it was the right thing to do. But I am being manipulated, I'm being prepared like a goose for dinner. I was not meant to be a messiah," he said softly.

Turning she looked at him and her eyes reflected the light of the torch, and for a moment he could not see her pupils. Her eyes seemed to glow like a cat's, and she appeared to be a stranger to him. "Perhaps you *were,* my husband. Perhaps you *are* the messiah!"

"You don't believe that. You *can't* believe it."

Miratrice looked down at her hands, began to wring them absently. "I don't know what I believe . . . I honestly don't."

He moved down beside her, held her in his arms, and

noticed that she was somewhat rigid, nervously tight. "I ask only that you believe in me."

Putting her head on his shoulder, she nodded silently. "All right. I'll try to do that."

"Good, now go to our quarters and make ready. You will need plenty of warm things for Bysshe. We will come for you at the appointed time."

Miratrice kissed him gently, stood and left the room. She was acting oddly, but Ozymandias had expected it. There was nothing in her catalogue of experiences which allowed her to deal with what was coming. He knew that she felt helpless and cut adrift from the only world she had ever known. He knew that the escape would be the most difficult task ever demanded of her, but he also felt that she would survive the ordeal. He believed in the love they had for each other, and he wanted to feel that it would be enough to weather whatever storms they might encounter.

CHAPTER 11

The night was like a glacier which crept across the hours with a deliberate slowness that would never end. Ozymandias had not given a thought to sleep as he paced about the "sickroom" waiting for the arrival of his companion. His mind switched from one topic to another with the quickness of a caged animal. A recurring question in his mind centered around the rush of events which had led him to this pivotal point in his life: How had everything happened so fast?

He had known that he would make mistakes as he grew older; it was part of gaining wisdom. The pages of the history books were littered with the chronicles of men's mistakes, and Ozymandias had not expected that he would escape the pattern. It was ironic, he thought, that the entire relationship between he and Kartaphilos revolved around the age-old philosophical argument—the benefits of experiential *vs.* intellectual knowledge. Kartaphilos and Ozymandias. Two forces, not especially opposed, but rather approaching the same goal from different directions. There were times when each of the two should be heeded, taking the advice or the judgment of the other. The trick, Ozymandias now knew, was knowing when to take advantage of each kind of knowledge . . .

A slight rapping at his door banished his thoughts.

Lifting the latch, he pulled back the door to see a familiar bearded face framed by the cowl of a gray robe.

"It is time," said Kartaphilos. "You are ready?"

Ozymandias nodded. "What about the guards? At the end of this corridor?"

"They will not grow old."

"You *killed* them?"

Kartaphilos shrugged. "I told you this might happen. They were not cooperative, and silence was necessary. Please, this is not the time to discuss ethical proprieties. We must be at the docks by sunrise. Miratrice is prepared?"

"In her room, waiting for us. With the child."

"Let's be off then."

The corridors of the Keep were dim and cold. Their shadows cast by the occasional oil lamp were long and misshapen as they moved along. Ozymandias's mind raced ahead, fearing what he might be forced to do. Only with a strong conscious effort could he calm himself, which he aided by taking slow, deep breaths. Their passage through the corridor, up the curling staircase to the upper rooms, was quiet and without event. When they reached the door to Miratrice's room, there was a crack of light at its bottom.

Rapping softly, they waited until she came to the door. "Is the child ready?" asked Ozymandias.

Miratrice nodded, and vanished for an instant back into the room, returning with the young boy in her arms. Ozymandias tried to look into her eyes, to give her some reassurance, but she seemed unable to return his comforting glance. Her expression belied her fear, her confusion and doubt.

"All right, we must move quickly now," said Kartaphilos, already walking quickly toward the descending stairwell.

Ozymandias guided his young wife and child while he brought up the rear. His heart was pounding as they crept down the cold stairs of darkness, descending to the lowest levels of the Keep where the catacombs and dungeons were. He attempted to remain calm so that he might employ an aspect of psychic powers—a little used, almost unconscious sense of the auras of others. It was a proximity sense, an ability which allowed him to know when others might be near before actually seeing or hearing them. Since he had not had much training in this sense, he often had difficulty differentiating the auras of those close about him and those who were actually beyond the range of the normal senses.

Kartaphilos had not expected there to be any guards in the lower chambers since there were few people who even knew about the escape passage out to the cliffs. And so it was a surprise when Ozymandias felt several extra waves of emanation ahead of him. The signals were weaker than those of the bodies directly ahead of them, and distant enough so that he could not discern how many there might be, but others were definitely ahead of them. Of that he was certain.

"Wait!" he whispered, taking hold of Miratrice's garment. Kartaphilos stopped, turned, looked at him.

"Bodies ahead of us," he said quickly. "Down, on the bottom level."

"How many?" Kartaphilos moved closer to him.

"Not sure. I thought this part of the Keep was usually deserted . . ."

"It is. This means only one thing—that they are waiting for us!"

"But how?" said Ozymandias. "How could they know?"

"It does not matter now," said Kartaphilos. "We have no choice at this point. They have probably closed in behind us, too. We have to go forward, and simply take them. I'll go first. Their weapons will have little effect on this alloy." The cyborg struck his chest lightly, turned, descended into the shadows.

Ozymandias moved ahead of Miratrice, motioning her to stay close behind him, and followed his companion. They completed the final turn to the catacomb floor and were faced with total darkness. His proximity sense was raging now, and there were many bodies ahead of them in the total blackness. He had to warn Kartaphilos! Had to make a move before they did!

"Hold!" a voice cut through the darkness, while someone struck a flint to an oil lamp.

In the instant of light, the image of the five guards printed itself on his retinas. Kartaphilos had already begun moving off to the left, raising his alloy arm like a war club; Ozymandias instinctively moved to the right.

There came a sound of metal thudding into flesh, the wheeze of breath being abruptly pounded from a set of lungs, and the clatter of a truncheon to the cold stone floor. Miratrice screamed as Ozymandias extended his right arm and concentrated on the power which he knew surged within his mind and body. Blue light began to dance about the tips of his fingers, casting an eerie, pale glow about the stunned faces of the guards who were still standing. Kartaphilos had poled one to the floor and was working on a second, while the other three remained huddled together as if hypnotized by the light at the end of Ozymandias's hand.

A bolt leaped from his hand, striking the nearest guard's pike. It became instantly hot, glowing a deep cherry red, before disintegrating into phosphoruslike fragments. The guard dropped to his knees, whimpering, as his two companions rushed forward. Again Ozymandias pointed his hand and the energy leaped forth, this time forking into two bolts which burned into the chest armor of the advancing men. Their screams shattered the darkness as they fell.

There was a moment of silence, punctuated only by the gasping breath of Miratrice. Then a spark of light, a warm glow as Kartaphilos fired the oil lamp. The dim light revealed five crumpled bodies, a clutter of weapons, and the looming frame of Kartaphilos above them.

"Good work," he said softly. "I don't know what you did, but it was quite effective. Now, quickly, we must hurry."

They moved quickly past the fallen men and located the stone panel, which swung back to reveal the passage to the cliff's face. The still, dank air of the catacombs was sucked past them, wrapped in the surly crosswinds which battered the sheer face of the promontory. The salty smell of the sea, the rankness of gull rookeries, the coolness of night, were all carried to them in an instant. There was a short, angled passage which opened upon the ledge itself—a narrow cut into the face of the cliff that was wide enough for only one person. The ledge formed a small platform, which, after several ems, became a crude case of descending stairs.

"Quickly, now," said Kartaphilos. "Stay close together! Lean in toward the face of the rock!"

Miratrice cringed as she approached the narrow ledge, unable to look over its edge to the darkness far below. The wind grabbed her robes and played with them roughly. Holding the child in one arm, she frantically reached out for her husband. "I can't do this! I have to go back!"

"You *can't* go back," cried Ozymandias, in an effort to be heard in the howl of the wind. He grabbed her arm sharply, knowing that he was hurting her soft flesh, and forced her ahead. Still she would not move forward, and Ozymandias lessened his grip upon her. "What's wrong? You must move. Just don't look *down!*"

Miratrice shook her head, and cradled the young child in her arms, looked down at him for a moment, then offered him to Ozymandias. "I can't carry him!" she said desperately. "I can't trust myself. Please, my husband. You must carry our son."

Ozymandias took the child from her, cradling his small body easily in his left arm. He nodded to her, and motioned her along, and this time she advanced slowly, keeping both hands against the cliff's face, leaning in and refusing to look over the ledge.

Kartaphilos continued in the lead, bounding down the stairs effortlessly, seemingly unaffected by the great height. He paused now and then to gauge the progress of Miratrice and Ozymandias, sometimes waiting, sometimes rushing downward. The wind pushed and pulled at them in capricious gusts, and balance was always a precarious thing. Ozymandias attempted to remain calm and employ his extrasensory abilities, but in the whine of the wind and the concentration required to gain firm purchase on the steps, it was a difficult task.

Thankfully, the moon was three quarters full, and its light was sufficient to see the steps. Ozymandias concentrated on the steps, the light, the restless child under his left arm. Beyond Miratrice, he watched Kartaphilos in the van, making steady progress. For a moment, a shadow crossed their path, and he was disoriented. It had been a cloudless night. There should have been nothing to interfere with the moonlight . . .

Kartaphilos was screaming out his name at the same instant he was looking for the source of the great shadow, and he cursed himself for not being more attuned to his proximity sense. Descending upon a cable was a large platform, a semicage carrying four archers and Beldamo. The sight was so absurd, so unexpected, that for a moment Ozymandias was stunned into immobility.

"Fools!" cried Beldamo, as he clung to the railing of the platform. The wind whipped about his long gray hair and his robes, and he appeared like a madman swinging back and forth in the crosswinds. The bowmen had strung their weapons and were taking aim. "Go back or be plucked from your perches!"

Miratrice moved closer to him and grabbed onto his shirt. "Go back, my sweet! Please! It is the only way!" Tears burst from her eyes, and she buried her face upon his shoulder.

"You can't keep us here, Beldamo!" he yelled, trying to buy time, trying to reason out the best course of action.

"How could you know?" cried Kartaphilos in an attempt to divide the sorcerer's attention.

Beldamo laughed as the platform inched lower, allowing the bowmen a better angle of shot. He shouted above the howling wind. "Don't you know that blood is far thicker than water?" And he laughed again.

Ozymandias grabbed Miratrice by the hair, pulling her face up to face him. His mind was torn by conflicting feelings of anger, disbelief.

"Why? Why, Miratrice?"

"For you, my love! For all of us! I couldn't tell you what madness I thought this plan. I tried to have us detained! You didn't understand! Everything will be all right, I promise you! Please, go back now. My grandfather will not harm you!"

"It's treachery!" cried Kartaphilos. "Don't listen to her!"

"Go back or I begin firing!" cried Beldamo.

He could not believe that Beldamo would risk injuring Miratrice or the child. It *had* to be an empty threat. No religious scheme could be more valuable than those lives. And yet the bowmen had taken their aims and pulled back their strings, and now only awaited a signal from the old man, who glared at them with wild, yellow eyes.

"You can't stop us, Beldamo!" cried Ozymandias, raising his right arm, pointing it at the swinging platform, as he summoned up his psychic energies.

The sorcerer laughed into the wind and threw up his

hands. Immediately a great amber glow surrounded the platform like St. Elmo's fire. A bolt of light jumped from Ozymandias's fingers, striking the glow and being absorbed into it like water into a sponge. The archers and Beldamo were unaffected.

"You dare attack me!" cried the wizard. "Stop them!"

The first volley of arrows was launched, one striking Kartaphilos in the shoulder with no effect. The three others clattered dangerously close to Ozymandias and his wife, but missed. His mind seethed with confusion and rage. It was impossible to believe what was happening, and he struggled to remain calm, to act with reason and plan.

He fired another bolt of energy at the platform and again it was repelled by the strange field of force which emanated from the sorcerer. The archers were readying new arrows, and it was only seconds before they would fire again.

Suddenly Kartaphilos launched what would follow into action. Leaping away from the face of the cliff he propelled his machine body at the platform, grabbing the railing with both hands. He impacted at the same moment the archers were loosing their bows, jarring their arms.

"Move downward! Now!" cried the cyborg. "I'll take care of them. Move!"

For an instant there was confusion on the platform as Beldamo and two of the archers reached down to dislodge Kartaphilos from his hanging perch. With one hand he held the railing in a steely grip, while he used his free hand as a club, striking the closest bowman and knocking him over the edge and into screaming darkness.

Ozymandias's heart soared for an instant at the incredible bravery of his friend and was torn between helping him and escaping. Miratrice screamed and pressed into him. The child squirmed dangerously within his blankets. One of the remaining archers had raised his bow and loosed a final arrow, but Ozymandias did not see it until it reached its target—the back of Miratrice's flowing robes.

Piercing her deeply, it forced her breath out and she could not even scream. Collapsing, her head fell back. Blood and pink foam bubbled from her slack lips; her eyes open but unseeing. He knew that she was already dead but still he cried out her name, fighting the incoherent rage and shock that burned blindly in him.

Looking up, he saw the shock and the insanity in the eyes of Beldamo. He had not planned for such a thing, and by now Kartaphilos had climbed over the rail, smashing the bodies of the two nearest archers, flinging the closest over the platform. The wind raged about the struggling figures, masking the screams of the dying men.

Without thinking, he lowered his wife's limp body to the steps, taking care to shield the child from further attack. Beldamo had turned to face him fully now. The wizard raised his hands and summoned up all his energies. He would strike Ozymandias from the face of the cliff like an insect. At the same instant Kartaphilos threw himself against the body of the last bowman, pushing him against Beldamo. All three fell into a heap at the edge of the platform, throwing it into an unbalanced swing which rocked close to the edge of the cliff.

Ozymandias knew what he must do, and leaped out into the darkness.

CHAPTER 12

The darkness rushed past him in a loud whisper and the sensation of falling was indistinct, almost dreamlike, and unconvincing. Summoning up his will, he concentrated upon the telekinetic powers which would brake his fall, levitate him and his son. He could feel the density of the earth below rushing toward him, but he could see nothing. And then there was the tug of an opposing force, slight at first, but gathering in intensity until it was gripping his body like a fist. He let his mind go with the flow of the force, taking it into his most inner core of being, feeding it, *becoming* the force.

The whisper of the descent was stilled, and he found himself hovering above the blackness of the earth. The only sound was the muted crush of the surf upon the breakers. Ozymandias drew a breath, exhaled slowly, and willed himself to descend slowly. Closer to the earth, the moonlight accented the rocks and indicated a safe place to touch down near the breakwater on a little used jetty. The docks were not far from the spot, and he would have to hurry to make the departure time.

Looking up, he strained to see the platform, and he wondered what might have happened to Kartaphilos. He paused but could see nothing against the shadows of the cliff and the overhang of Beldamo's Keep. Whatever had taken place was still wrapped in the darkness of the dying night.

Young Bysshe had begun to cry and wriggle in his blan-

kets, but there was no time to attend to him. Ozymandias
moved quickly down the jetty and picked out the fastest
route to the docks. As he walked, a new calmness entered
him and the adrenaline overflow from the encounter seeped
away. He became aware of his pounding heart, the roaring
in his inner ears, the tightness in the muscles of his jaw,
neck, and shoulders.

Miratrice. The image of the arrow piercing her, the
quickly spreading stain upon her robes, her eyes looking at
him but not seeing—it was as though her death had been a
dream, a fantasy that he could not accept. It had happened
so quickly, so surrealistically, that it was as if it had not
happened at all. As he walked on, the pain in his chest
began to grow until it was no longer a dull throb but a
lance of fire, which seared and licked at his soul. For the
first time, Ozymandias thought he understood the pain of
loss, the shock of death, and the message of mortality that
touches everyone. It was a pain so sharp and so real that he
could not imagine how humans had endured it, unending,
for so many millennia. *Miratrice.* Her name repeated itself
in his mind, endlessly, and he struggled to accept that she
no longer existed . . .

. . . and it was not until he saw the running lanterns of
the ships, heard the slap of the incoming tide against their
hulls, that he realized how far he had come. Moving
quickly from pier to pier, he searched out the *Hidden
Dream* and its handsomely paid captain. The first beacons
of dawn were searchlighting the eastern horizon, and he
knew that time grew short. There were a fair number of
freighters still loading at the piers ahead of him, and if he
had to approach each one, he might miss the departure. He
did not want to risk asking one of the stevedores for fear of
being recognized, but there was little choice.

A short, stocky man, busy hefting bales of Gnarran wool
and too busy to take notice of Ozymandias, directed him to

the *Hidden Dream* and returned to his task. Carrying the now sleeping Bysshe in the folds of the blankets, Ozymandias walked quickly to the appropriate pier and headed for the *Dream*'s gangway.

"Yo! State your business," said the first mate, who stood on deck, holding a cargo manifest in his gnarled hands.

"I am booked for passage to Borat, along with a man called Kartaphilos."

The mate checked his lists, and nodded. "Party of four?" He looked up questioningly.

Ozymandias swallowed, fighting the tightness in his throat. "Yes, originally. One of the others has been delayed, and the fourth—the fourth will not be coming with us."

"Change of plans at the last minute, eh?"

Ozymandias nodded. "Yes, a—a change of plans."

"All right then, come aboard. Cabins are down the ladder under the fo'c'sle. We shove off as soon as the last of the cargo's aboard. Your friend better be quick about his business or we'll be under weigh."

Ozymandias nodded and made his way across the deck, avoiding the clutter of ropes, fittings, and unstashed bales of wool. As he descended the ladder and sought out his cabin, he wondered what had become of Kartaphilos, and smiled ironically at the mate's reference to his companion's 'business.' It was quite a business . . .

The bunks in the cabin were small and cramped, tucked away into the bulkheads to conserve on space, and without the amenities of even so sparse a place as Beldamo's Keep. Gently, he placed the sleeping child on the lower bunk, and wrapped the blankets more tightly about his small body. He was grateful that the boy would not remember the trauma and the pain that had been generated around him that early morning. Staring into the small child's face, Ozymandias was charmed by the perfect serenity of the portrait. He wondered what it would be like to be so small and so untouched by the realities of the world, and despite what he knew about the rigors of childhood and the psychological agonies to be endured in the maturation process, he regretted not having had the opportunity to experience them. In that sense, he imagined that he might not be a whole man, a complete person, and he hoped that it would not be to his detriment.

He tried not to consider what he would be doing in Zend Avesta without the guidance and experience of Kartaphilos, and he refused to believe that the cyborg was dead. He kept thinking that he would hear footsteps in the outer corridor, turn, and see the scraggly gray beard, the hooded robe, the sardonic grin.

But it was not meant to be, and soon he heard orders being shouted above decks, and the groan of wood, the snap of lines being thrown, and the slap of the tide against the hull as the *Hidden Dream* left the docks. He remained in the cabin, watching his sleeping child, using his training to remain calm, to attempt to rationally review the proceedings of the last several days. There was much to think upon, and much to understand about the experience of life. Perhaps the solitude and quiet of the cruise would give him the time to reconcile the new changes in his life, assist him in directing what his destiny might be.

When he thought back to how idealistic he had been when he first came to human consciousness at the Citadel, he smiled. He had wanted to be a herald, an educator, and an inspiration to humankind. Now it seemed so grandiose, so unrealistic. Ozymandias had not expected how humankind would react to the offering of himself; he had not known then that even the most benign intentions might be perverted.

He was not aware of how time had been passing while he had been lost in his thoughts, and at first he did not hear the gentle rap upon the cabin door. Turning, he told who-ever it was to enter.

The oak panel swung in, and a tall, lean, but obviously muscular man stood at the threshold. He had gray hair, a large drooping mustache, and goggle-like spectacles—ob-viously a product of Zend Avesta. He wore the traditional blue canvas running gear of a sailor, but his braided cap indicated his rank.

"I'm Captain Sontorges," he said extending his hand. "Welcome aboard the *Hidden Dream*. I'm afraid Kar-taphilos did not make ship."

"So I gathered. Did you know him well?"

The captain shrugged. "How well do you know any man you meet in a tavern? I know that I liked as much of him as I got to know. What happened to him?"

"I'm not sure," said Ozymandias, wondering whether or not this man should be confided in. "He was delayed and will probably have to make passage on another ship."

"That may be difficult," said Sontorges.

"Why?"

"The shipping lanes between the isle and points south-west, primarily to Zend Avesta, are getting too risky for most vessels. Last word I received, the Behistar has broken the Interdict and has declared war on the rest of us—again. We should flatten the bastards this time and be done with them, that's what I say."

"Do you anticipate trouble?"

"Not likely," said the Captain. "The *Dream*'s a big ship. We've got our own cannon, and I doubt if there's a Behis-tar raider big enough to want to lock horns with us on the open sea. Their habit is to take the smaller ships, ones that can be fitted for fighting and speed."

Ozymandias could not think of anything to say for a mo-ment, and simply stared at the captain, who was also silent, and seemed to be studying his passenger unabashedly.

"Is there something wrong?" Ozymandias broke the silence, which was growing uncomfortable.

"Not really," said Sontorges. "I was just wondering why you had to escape the isle . . ."

"What makes you think we were escaping?"

The captain smiled and shook his head. "I've been a seaman for more than thirty years. You think you're the first fugitives I've ever shipped?"

"You still haven't answered my question."

"All right, look at you—you come aboard with no belongings but the clothes on your back, a baby wrapped in some rags, and looking like you've had some kind of tussle with somebody. And if I'm not getting senile, I'd say that's dried blood on the sleeve of your tunic there. You could be a murderer, a kidnapper, a political prisoner, anything at all—"

"And you don't mind?"

"Kartaphilos has already paid me."

"And you are a merchant above all else, is that correct? You are above, or shall I say, outside of, all moral judgments?"

"I try to be. My country is the open sea, and I pledge no allegiances to any of these scrappers who call themselves governments. No, I don't rightly care who you are, or what you are. At least not yet anyway."

"Meaning?"

"Meaning that I may get interested later, if it pays me to do so." Captain Sontorges stood up and moved to the door. "It was nice talking to you, sir. I'd stay but I have to get us piloted out and away from the reefs. Oh, and by the way, your . . . 'museum piece' is safely stowed below. I suppose you'll be wanting it unloaded at Borat?"

Ozymandias had forgotten about the 'crawler, and for a moment did not understand the reference. After a slight pause, he answered. "Yes. That was the original agreement, was it not?"

The captain nodded, smiled, and touched the brim of his cap before closing the door behind him. Ozymandias had picked up an instant dislike for the man more out of instinct than anything else. It was a matter of trust, and the manner in which he spoke. There was a boldness in Sontorges that seemed to imply that he was challenging Ozymandias to attempt to stop him from doing whatever he pleased.

The voyage might not prove as peaceful as he had first imagined.

CHAPTER 13

Although the passage to Zend Avesta was not long, Ozymandias appreciated the time-consuming duties necessary to care for a small child. Having no prior experience in the task, he had to rely on what little information there had been on the subject in Guardian's memory files, the use of common sense and a dash of human instinct. The ship's cabin boy was helpful and, surprisingly, so were several of the younger crewmen. It seemed that the presence of a baby on the ship was a great novelty to the men, and they looked forward to playing with the child as a relief from the tedium of the voyage. It was also during this time that Ozymandias developed a closeness, an intimacy, with his son that had not been there before. It seemed that Miratrice had sheltered the child from contact with others in her efforts to be a perfect mother—even to the exclusion of the father. Ozymandias would often look down into the boy's bright blue young eyes and marvel at the miracle of life and how he had helped to create this miniature of himself. He looked forward to the day when the boy would no longer be a silent, helpless creature, but actually a companion with whom he could share his impressions and experiences.

But that would be far off in the future, he knew. The first thing Ozymandias did when he reached Borat was to locate a reputable monastery and make the necessary arrangements for the child's keep. He required a place of warmth and understanding, a place which would raise the child in an environment of intellectual fervor and true enlightenment. The monastery which fit these requirements was the Abbey of the Order of St. Brel, which was located in the center of the teeming city of Borat. Not known for its religious inclinations, the state of Zend Avesta supported only those spiritual institutions which were enlightened enough to recognize the value of technology and invention. Hence the Order of St. Brel comprised a host of enterprising monks who worked hand in hand with the state's finest scientific minds. In fact, many of Avesta's leading thinkers and inventors had received their education at the respected abbey.

The monks' respect for science made their acceptance of Ozymandias and young Bysshe more easily accomplished with the arrival of the landcrawler. The monks recognized immediately that the machine was no museum piece and were anxious to study the mechanisms in an effort to perhaps duplicate it. If they could produce and market such a machine, the holy coffers would indeed swell, and therefore make more funds available with which to spread the word of God—whatever that might be.

Time passed within the walls of the abbey, and while Ozymandias had no desire to take up the habit of the monks, he did find certain aspects of their life appealing. They seemed content to do the work of God and investigate the mysteries of His world. The pursuit and recording of knowledge was a sweet passion for them, and they went about the task with an enthusiasm that was natural and absent of the ritualistic pyrotechnics of the cultists of Gnarra.

The war which Kartaphilos had foreseen was drawing close to explosive fruition, however, and the governments of the World were finally getting together on what course of action should be taken. It seemed as if Zend Avesta had been selected as the multinational army's quartermaster, having drawn the job of developing and manufacturing weapons and supplies for the defeat of the Behistar Republic. There was much talk of the coming conflict, and Ozymandias soon grew weary of the catchphrase manner in which the conflict was viewed, even by the saintly monks. He did not refuse them, however, when they sought his assistance in the development of new weapons—a talent at which he, of course, was quite adept.

It was not long after his involvement with the monastery's technicians that he began to gather about him a reputation as a supertalented scientist. Soon, technicians from other factories, scientists and professors from the universities, and even government defense ministers sought him out for advice and ideas. It was at this time that he wished Kartaphilos could be with him for the advice and the clarity of perception that marked the cyborg so well. Ozymandias had jumped into the projects of warmasters so completely that he thought he might be losing sight of his original objectives. His major problem, it appeared, was that he adopted the projects and interests of whomever he became associated with, working with the enthusiasm and sincerity of a young child, which, when he considered his true chronological age, he actually was.

Realizing this about himself, he should not have been surprised when the representatives of Avestan government summoned him to testify before the Senate in the capital city of Ques'ryad.

But, in his naïveté, he was indeed surprised.

He was accompanied to the great Avestan city by several monks from the abbey who served as escorts and bodyguards. This was necessary because the news of Ozymandias's trip spread before him and the enlightened populace of the loosely structured democracy filled the village streets to catch a glimpse of the famous scientist and arms genius. *Look on my works, ye Mighty, and despair,* thought Ozymandias, realizing how oddly prophetic the line of poetry had become.

The landcar in which they traveled did not pause once entering Ques'ryad, and he did not have much of an opportunity to view what was easily the most advanced, most sophisticated city in the entire World. Its skyline was a vast array of spires and towers, bridges and elevated tramways. It was a city of motion and direction, of color and light and purpose.

As to exactly what purposes, Ozymandias was not informed completely; otherwise, he would not have walked so simply into the hands of the Avestan Senate. Their quarters were contained within a large cube-shaped building called the Blockhouse, which was functionally designed and built to withstand the heaviest attacks possible from an invading army.

The Senate Hall was a semicircular amphitheater which held seating for the entire assembly of representatives—fifty in all—plus a central dais and speaker's platform. When Ozymandias was escorted into the Senate chambers, he could see that all the seats were occupied, including the dais and a small spectators' gallery off to the side. A murmur slowly spread throughout the room as he entered and was shown to a chair before a table which faced the dais, plus the seven black-robed men who sat before it.

A tall, thin man with sunken cheeks and dark eyes stood up at the dais, flanked by three others on each side. He looked down at Ozymandias for a moment without speaking, then motioned to the assembly and the gallery that he required silence. The murmuring subsided, and the man prepared to speak.

"Ozymandias, welcome to the Assembly of the Senate of

Zend Avesta. I am Senior Member Brokaw, chairman of the ruling body. I will come directly to the point of your summons before us: we know who you are."

A jolt passed through Ozymandias, but he did not allow it to change his calm expression. It was quite possible that the Senate only *thought* they knew who he was.

"I'm afraid I don't understand, Your Honor," he said slowly.

"The news of your accomplishments at the abbey and in some of Borat's laboratories had not gone unnoticed here in Ques'ryad. You underestimate our sophistication by coming here and not expecting to be investigated. If there is one center of information and research capability in the entire World, then it is here in Zend Avesta. In fact, we were first informed of your odd nature the day you arrived in Borat with your 'museum piece,' as you call it."

"By Captain Sontorges, no doubt?"

The chairman smiled and nodded. "Yes, a good ship's captain seeks revenue from whatever source is willing to volunteer it. We deal in information at the Senate, and one of the finest sources of data has always been perceptive men of the sea."

"Still, you have told me nothing surprising. In fact, I expected it, and I hide nothing from you. My name is Ozymandias, and I have offered my services to the war effort . . ."

Chairman Brokaw smiled again. "Yes, that is true, but the story is somewhat incomplete, wouldn't you say?"

"Why don't you tell me."

Brokaw sighed. "Very well, I shall. It was a simple matter to trace your past back to the Isle of Gnarra, where it seems you have established quite a reputation for yourself. Even now in the streets of every village on the isle, you are referred to as the Last Prophet. From the reports we have gathered, you are obviously well adept in psychic abilities, as well as having an inordinate amount of knowledge about First Age technology and history. Combine these facts with the reports from the Eleusynnian authorities about a mysterious healer and parkside orator, and we have a more complete portrait of Ozymandias, do we not?"

"You seem to know where I have been, and some of the things I have accomplished, but that does not guarantee that you understand my identity," he said in a loud voice, which was intended to show the chairman that he was not intimidated. Inwardly, however, he was impressed by the extent of the knowledge the Senate had compiled on him. His only question was how much more they knew, and what they intended to do with him.

Again the chairman smiled. "Perhaps you are not aware of how well kept our records are in Ques'ryad?"

"No. I am not. Is there anything else?"

The chairman cleared his throat, referred to a sheaf of papers before him, then began speaking. "Oh, yes, a few pieces of data which are quite fascinating—the first being your 'gift' to the Museum of Technology in Borat, the landcrawler. Not only is its presence mentioned in the report from Eleusynnia, which definitely confirms your presence there, but also the device has been examined by our finest scientists, and their conclusion is that it is indeed a First Age machine."

Ozymandias shifted position in his chair. "That should not be surprising. It is nothing more than what I claimed it to be. I am not the first to have discovered First Age artifacts in working condition."

"No, you are certainly not. And that is not my point. In fact, since you mention it, there was once a very famous explorer in our country, who was originally from the mining districts of Hadaan. His name was Stoor, and he made his reputation on being able to retrieve First Age artifacts. Does that name sound familiar to you?"

Ozymandias nodded silently, unable to speak. They had
made all the proper connections, and it had unnerved him
greatly. He felt as though he were standing naked before a
large crowd.

Chairman Brokaw nodded forcefully, smiling as he
looked out upon the gathered members of the Senate.
"Yes, I thought the name would be *very* familiar. It figures
quite prominently in a historical document known as the
Hamer Notebooks. Are you familiar with the document?"

"No, I am not."

"Let me refresh your memory. The document was written by a seaman known as Varian Hamer, a man who accompanied Stoor of Hadaan on what proved to be his most
famous expedition. Hamer has recorded an incredible adventure in his Notebooks, an adventure which mentions the
existence of a First Age fortress called the Citadel, a
cyborg warrior who calls himself Kartaphilos, and a machine intelligence called Guardian. Let me read you something, Ozymandias . . ."

The chairman flipped through the pages on his desk for
a moment, then picked up one sheet from the others. "This
is from one of the final entries in the Notebooks: 'The
great machine, now relieved of the burden of conscience it
had carried for more than two thousand years, offered itself
up to us with a single condition. Knowing that it contained
the secrets of the First Age, Kartaphilos felt that it would
be instrumental in rebuilding the World into what it had
once been. The Guardian was agreeable to this if Kartaphilos would attempt what seems to me an impossible
task.

"'And yet, Kartaphilos did not seem put off by the
Guardian's request, and went straight to work in carrying it
out. The mere mention of the idea and my inability to accept or comprehend it only demonstrates the powers and
the vision of the builders of the First Age. I do not know if

Guardian's wish is within the scope of Kartaphilos, but they will attempt it, regardless of the outcome.

"'The thing which Guardian requested was both flattering and horrifying: it wished to become *human.*'"

The chairman paused for a moment as he lay the paper upon his desk top, all the while staring at Ozymandias. "The emphasis on the last word is mine," he said softly. "An interesting document, is it not?"

"Fascinating," said Ozymandias.

"Are we safe in assuming that the Kartaphilos mentioned in the Notebooks is the same as your companion and partner in adventure in G'Rdellia and the Isle of Gnarra?"

"Yes," said Ozymandias. "He is the same person."

"Very interesting. Did you know that the document goes on to sketchily describe biological experiments and techniques which Kartaphilos attempted? Our scientists believe that the cyborg was trying to grow a human body for the machine intelligence called Guardian—and that he *succeeded.* It is further believed that you, Ozymandias, are the product of that success. Do you deny it?"

Chairman Brokaw's words seemed to echo through the amphitheater, and Ozymandias stood mutely, for an instant not able to believe that the Avestans had cracked his secret so easily. Not even the shrewd Kartaphilos could have expected such a neat, almost effortless compilation of the facts.

"Ozymandias, you have not answered me. Do you deny that you are the embodiment of the machine intelligence? Were you once the Guardian machine mentioned in the Hamer Notebooks?"

He looked up at the dais, at the expressionless faces of the Senate officials, feeling as though he were on trial for a terrible offense. A feeling of guilt swept through him, even though he knew he had no reason to feel guilty.

"No, I deny nothing," he said slowly. "I was once called Guardian, yes. Are you satisfied now?"

The chairman smiled. "Please, there is no reason to be antagonistic. We sought only the truth, and you should not fault us for that. In fact, what you have accomplished is truly a miraculous feat, something far beyond the scope of our own culture's understanding, and we admire you greatly for it. I am certain that you have gathered up a wealth of experiences in the process that have no equal, and the Senate of Zend Avesta congratulates you wholeheartedly."

Ozymandias grinned. "I suppose I should say thank you."

"That is your prerogative. But are you not curious to know why we have summoned you here to verify our suspicions?"

"I have my own ideas as to what is motivating you, but I will wait on them. No doubt you wish to tell me in your own words."

Chairman Brokaw nodded graciously. "Before you pass judgment on our motives prematurely, I think you should consider the phenomenon of your existence in the objective sense. From your earliest public appearances, disregarding the popular notions and impressions of your power, *any* intelligent mind would see you for what you are—an instrument of immense knowledge, power, and manipulation. The authorities in Eleusynnia hunted you because they recognized, quite quickly, that you were a special individual. In times of unrest and misguided development such as these, the populations which all the governments oversee are unstable masses. The common people need stability and purpose, they need to share in the vision of their appointed rulers, and sadly, they often do not have the intellectual ability to do so. When this is the case, a wise government will replace the actual goals and visions of the state with something symbolic, something which the masses may understand and rally about. Charismatic figures have always been very adept in the creation of populist symbols, even if they must *become* the symbol itself. Do you see my point?"

"Yes, it is quite clear."

"Thank you," said Brokaw. "To continue, I may cite the plans of the mystics of the Isle of Gnarra. Your presence in their culture conformed well enough to their mythologies that they attempted to use you as a focal point, a gathering force to unify their people, and begin the spiritual renaissance which had been sadly lacking in their isolated society. They saw you as the kind of leader they needed to reclaim their place in the forefront of global society, and you cannot fault them for their misguided plans, especially when you consider the stakes for which they played the game.

"I can assure you that if you had traveled to any of the half dozen other countries about the gulf, you would have been appraised in a similar light. You are a *special* person, Ozymandias, and only a *fool* would not recognize the potential *power* and wisdom you represent! And I am not talking about your crowd-pleasing tricks, but rather about the long-term effects of your very existence: the potential for education, edification, invention, rediscovery, and not to mention the gene pool in your body which could be the progenitor of a new race of gifted humans. You are, in the words of the Tshar of the Shudrapur Dominion, 'a potential national treasure.' I might add that the rulers of virtually every country in the gulf have by now heard of your exploits, and covet you in their courts . . ."

Ozymandias looked down for a moment, drew a breath. For a few seconds, he considered summoning up some of the power that Brokaw had been discussing to free himself from the unpleasant atmosphere of the Senate. It was conceivable that he could effect an escape, but he had no desire to again be on the run, especially when he had the welfare of his son to consider. No, he thought. An escape would have to be planned ahead of time. Better to endure this inquisition now. There would be time later.

"Are you listening to me?" asked Chairman Brokaw.

"Yes, I was merely considering your words. There is not much I can say in reply, you know, other than that I suppose you are asking me to take a position within your government, or something similar to that."

"You suppose correctly, Ozymandias. From this day forward, you should consider yourself a 'national treasure' of Zend Avesta. You will be serving the nation in the capacity of Science Advisor, Military Attaché, and Assistant to the Prime Minister. Please do not be put off by the officiousness of the titles; they are to please the constituency only. In reality, you will be the servitor of the state in whatever capacity it so chooses. Do you understand?"

"I think so. I am henceforth at your beck and call, a *slave* for all practical purposes, I will be expected to sit calmly and allow my brain to be picked clean of all facts, abilities, and ideas, is that correct?"

The chairman frowned for a moment, then smiled once again. "Your choice of words is rather severe, yet I find them accurate enough, yes."

"And what makes you feel that I would in any way comply with such a scheme? Do you think that I have no scruples, no ideals, no feelings of my own? What makes you think that I would agree to your own personal view of how the World's affairs should be conducted? Do you think you are dealing with a child?"

The chairman chuckled softly. "It is ironically amusing that you should phrase our situation so aptly."

Ozymandias understood immediately what the chairman was implying. "What have you done with my son? You bastards! You stinking bastards!"

The chairman raised his right hand, gestured for silence.

"Do not be alarmed. Your son is perfectly safe, and will remain so as long as you cooperate with us. Please understand that we are reasonable men, civilized men, and wish to do no harm to a young child. But being civilized, we have a very clear understanding of the ways of the World, and in essence it is a world of merchants, of barterers, and there are few instances in which one does not receive something in return for something else. In this case, you will serve the state in return for the safety of your only son."

"I can't believe this," said Ozymandias so softly that it was as though he were thinking aloud. His thoughts were so confused, so jumbled by the realization of his predicament, so angered that he could have acted so foolishly, and with such blind trust.

"Ah, but you must believe it. It is a simple bargain which we offer. Surely it is not a terribly demanding decision you must make."

"Where is my son?"

"He has been taken from the abbey. In fact, he was taken only hours after you left for your journey to Ques'ryad. I am not at liberty to divulge the location of his safekeeping, but I can tell you this: that he is being given the finest of care, and is completely safe; and also that any attempts on your part to find him would be totally fruitless. If you refuse to cooperate with us in any way, you will never see your son again. It is that simple."

"You insensitive bastards! How can you do such a thing?"

"Oh, please, Ozymandias. Please spare us the melodrama. Don't you realize that we are dealing with the future destiny of the World itself? Is it reasonable for men of wisdom and forethought to be concerned about the life of one child or the feelings of one man, when contrasted against the fates of millions of people for generations to come? If you think about it, you will see that it is a small price to pay for the greater good of humankind. Your work for Zend Avesta will benefit the entire human race—and is that not the purpose to which you had planned to devote your life?"

Ozymandias did not reply as he stood trying to order his thoughts, to regain rational control of his raging emotions. It was indeed ironic that the chairman would emphasize the service to civilization they wished of him. It *was* his centermost hope that he could benefit humankind, but he had not expected things to work out as they were beginning to.

Looking up, he addressed the chairman. "I will need time to . . . think about all this. I would like to know more specifically what will be expected of me."

"I have arranged for you to meet with various government officials, chiefs of staff, leaders from various disciplines, who will brief you on our overall plans. This can begin as soon as possible, if you wish."

"And what about my private life? Or am I to be totally deprived of one? Will I be a prisoner of the state?"

"Of course not. Zend Avesta is an enlightened democracy. You shall be provided with every amenity of civilization, and shall be free to go about our country at your leisure. Bear in mind, however, that you will be kept under constant surveillance, and that despite your freedom of movement, if the state feels that you are showing evidence of an attempt to locate your son, drastic measures will be taken. Is that clear?"

"Yes, it is perfectly clear. I will need time to consider all this. Will I be able to see my son?"

"Eventually, but for now, I am afraid that will be out of the question."

"Then how will I know that he is safe? How will I know you plan to keep your part of the bargain?"

"You will be forced to trust us in the beginning. Once we are satisfied that you are indeed cooperating with the state, we will arrange visitation schedules, which will be conducted under the tightest security controls you can imagine. Please, Ozymandias, take as much time as you will require. We are confident that it will not take very long for you to make your decision. We have arranged a suite of rooms for you in the Ministry Buildings—a place usually reserved for the most respected guests of the state. If you have nothing more to add, I will arrange for you to be escorted there."

He said nothing for a moment, gathering his thoughts about him, trying to think rationally, calmly. There was no use in becoming excited or excessively outraged. There *had* to be alternatives. There had to be other solutions to the situation. He kept telling himself that all he needed was time to consider the possibilities.

The chairman cleared his throat. "Ozymandias . . . is there anything further you wish to say?"

"No. Nothing at this time. I would like to go now, if you please."

The chairman nodded, and signaled for his escort. He was taken from the chambers of the Senate and driven to the Ministry Buildings, where his quarters had been prepared. It was easily the most lavish accommodations he had ever encountered, but he was in no mood to appreciate the decor or the service. Visions of his young son kept intruding upon his thoughts, and he knew that he had no real decision to make.

He felt so foolishly naïve, so unprepared to play with the true Powers in the World. All his dreams had been destroyed so quickly, it seemed, and his expectations of life had been so unrealistic, so filled with romantic idealism, that he could think of himself as nothing but a failure.

He needed time to think. There was no time, and there was all of time.

CHAPTER 14

In spite of the unpleasant associations connected with Ques'ryad, Ozymandias could not deny that it was a breathtakingly alive city. Its boulevards and avenues were always filled with traffic, its shops and marketplaces abuzz with the languages of the World, its parks and gardens ablaze with the colors of flowers and flags, banners and heralds of every tribe and nation. It was an urban crossroads of commerce, discovery, and political maneuvering. Its architecture was the most modern in the World, its ships and vehicles the sleekest, its technology the brightest.

A week had passed in the great city, and Ozymandias had spent the majority of the time alone. Each day, a courier from the Senate would contact him, and he sent the man back each time with the short message that he was still considering the proposal. In fact, he was not considering anything. He had known from the beginning that he would be forced to accept the terms of the bargain, or allow his son to be killed. He knew that a father does not have to think about such a thing.

The only thing he had accomplished in that week was to prolong the inevitable, to put off working for the state of Zend Avesta. His meetings with the various government leaders had revealed the overall plan of the state quite clearly and simply. They honestly believed that technology was the answer to the majority of the World's problems, and since Zend Avesta was easily the most advanced country in the known World, they believed it was only fitting that their nation should lead the remainder of the World back to a proper level of civilization.

The first order of business, of course, was to assemble a sophisticated, mechanized army which could rapidly and effectively annihilate the barbarian hordes to the east—the rag-and-bone kulaks from the Behistar Republic. After which the rest of the World would have no choice but to bend to the will of so great a military force. There would be a minimum of violence, just a bit of healthy, loud sword rattling. Most of the leaders felt that this would be enough to guarantee cooperation from the other gulf countries. What followed would be large-scale plans to industrialize the underdeveloped countries and organize lanes of commerce and communication. Transportation systems would have to be built, then wholesale construction and organization could begin. The entire economy of the gulf would be resurrected and fueled by the endless list of construction projects being created in Zend Avesta. In short, the national leaders envisioned a technological renaissance, inspired and administered by the figure of Ozymandias.

If there were not the extenuating circumstances of his son's captivity, Ozymandias would have actually been pleased with the grand plan, despite its grandiose notions and the First Age testament to the dangers of an overly technocratic society.

But under the conditions of his "employment," he had no interest in the destiny of civilization.

The only incident which brightened his outlook occurred at the end of his first week in Ques'ryad. While taking a solitary walk through one of the urban gardens which accented the wide boulevards of the city, he found his only friend, Kartaphilos.

Looking like an old man, dressed in his familiar hooded robe, the cyborg was seated beside an elaborate fountain. To any passerby, he appeared to be nothing more than an

old man, a foreigner perhaps, resting and meditating upon
the beauty of the day. Ozymandias rushed up to him, unable to contain the joy which surged through him. He called
out his friend's name as he ran, breaking into a wide,
laughing smile when Kartaphilos turned and recognized
him.

"I don't believe it's you! I can't believe I've found you!
Are you all right? What happened to you in Gnarra? How
long have you been here?"

Kartaphilos raised his hand softly. "Please my friend.
One question at a time."

"I'm sorry. It's just that I am so shocked to see you here.
And there's been very little to be happy about. Perhaps I'm
just overreacting."

"No, I doubt that. I came here from the abbey in Borat.
It was there that I learned what they have done to you. I'm
sorry . . ."

Ozymandias looked away for a moment. "Yes, well,
we'll have to deal with that eventually. We will have time
to talk, but not right now, please. Tell me what happened
to you. The last time I saw you, things looked quite grim."

Kartaphilos smiled and nodded his head. "Yes, it *was*
grim, wasn't it?"

"Well, what happened?"

"Let me see . . . The last I saw of you, you had taken a
leap into the darkness, having great faith in your abilities.
At that point I was finishing off the last of the archers. Beldamo was half crazed by that time, and was in no position
to summon up his own telekinetic powers. It was simply a
matter of picking him up and heaving him off the platform."

"So he is dead, too . . ." Ozymandias shook his head
slowly.

"Did you expect anything less?"

"No, I suppose not." Ozymandias looked at his friend. "I

think that the more I learn about this World, the less I am in favor of it."

"That's true enough, but unfortunately, it is the only one we've got."

"But go on, please. After you cleared the platform, then what?"

Kartaphilos shrugged. "A little pendulum action got the whole rig swinging enough so that I could regain a position on the staircase. I retrieved Miratrice's body and carried it down to the village, where I made arrangements for her funeral services. Under the circumstances, it was the best I could do, and I did not know how you felt about such things . . ."

Ozymandias paused for a moment, thinking of his dead wife, imagining Kartaphilos bearing her lifeless form through the darkness. An ache shot through his heart, and he felt tears in the corners of his eyes. "Funerals? I don't know," he said with an effort. "I guess that I never thought much about them. They are more for the living than the dead, don't you think?"

"I agree, but I did not know what else to do. It was *she* who betrayed us, you know . . ."

"I don't know if betrayal is the right word. She did what she believed was best for me. She just did not understand. That is the trouble with everyone: no one seems to understand anything about anyone else."

"I see that you are continuing to learn about us . . ."

"You speak as though we are all a collection of aliens," said Ozymandias.

Kartaphilos nodded dramatically. "Yes, perhaps we are —each an alien to the other." He paused and looked out to the fountain, beyond it to the skyline of the city. "And yet, we are capable of things like this . . ." He gestured at the sweeping architecture, the graceful lines of Ques'ryad.

"We are capable of anything," said Ozymandias. "That is what is most inspiring and most frightening."

"You have become jaded, my friend."

"There's plenty of time to discuss my state of mind, but if I may be honest with you, I don't think I'm in the mood to do it right now. I would prefer to hear something simple. Finish your tale of adventure. I need something vicarious."

"There is not much left to tell," said Kartaphilos. "When I left the village for the docks, your ship had already sailed. An alarm had been sounded at the Keep, and the militia was being summoned. It was too early for anyone to know what had happened, or to know that Beldamo had been killed, but I knew that the news would travel fast. It would have been hazardous to remain in the village, so I headed inland to cross the mountains in the center of the isle, in the hope that I might arrive at one of the western port villages before word of the disaster in Hern . . ."

"Did you?"

"Just barely. Two days' hard traveling brought me to Taurin, which is a fairly good sized town on the gulf. Already there were rumors circulating of political unrest on the east coast of the isle, but no one seemed to have all the details at that time. No names were being mentioned, although many of the people expressed concern for the fate of their newest member of the Innermost Circle. I jumped a freighter bound for Mentor, stayed there until I could arrange for a ship to Borat. When I arrived there less than three days ago, I began a systematic search of the monasteries, convents, and seminaries, hoping that I would find you.

"I knew there was something wrong immediately. As soon as I began making inquiries, I was greeted with mixed reactions of fear, outrage, and feigned ignorance. Faced with a total information blackout, I was forced to go to the only place where information flows as freely as the beverages. In the smoke-filled halls of the harbor taverns, I finally pieced together what had happened to you. The monks of St. Brel were close-mouthed and more than fearful of my presence at the abbey . . ."

"Bysshe? Did you hear anything about my son?"

Kartaphilos shook his head. "Only that he was not there, and had been taken away by the authorities."

"Could you find him? Could *we* find him?"

Kartaphilos shrugged. "That is difficult to say. From what I have heard, you are going to be kept quite busy. I would say your chances of locating the boy are practically nothing."

"I have already agreed to cooperate, in my mind, that is. I have just been stalling for time. Waiting, but not knowing for what I was waiting. Maybe for you, Kartaphilos. Maybe I *knew* that you would show up eventually."

"Perhaps you did."

"Is there anything that we can do?"

"I don't know. I think that at least for the time, you should cooperate with them. As for me, I think it would be safest if I maintained a low profile. If the state decides that I am a problem, they may imprison me, or even eliminate me."

"We are probably being watched right now," said Ozymandias. "I don't feel anything with my proximity sense, but they may still be in the area."

"I am certain of it."

"But I don't want to put you into danger. If you think it is hopeless, then get away while you can. They already have the ultimate leverage on me, but I don't think they would be beyond using it on you, too. If they feel you could be useful to them, even if only to dissect you, to make more like you."

Kartaphilos smiled. "They would have to catch me first. I still have a few tricks left. They might wish they had not tried."

Ozymandias looked around the park, searching the cool greenery for any sign of Avestan agents. That he could neither see them nor sense them bothered him greatly. He exhaled slowly. "Then what do we do?"

"Go back, and tell them that you will comply. I will make every effort to locate your son. If I can do that, then we may have a chance to move against them. You have no other choices at this point."

Ozymandias stood up, not facing his friend but staring absently up at the deep blue sky. "What you say is not very encouraging, but it is all that we have. All right, I will go to them and wait until I hear from you."

"Good-bye, my friend."

"How will you get in touch with me?"

Kartaphilos chuckled. "I am sure that the art of the bribe lives even in Zend Avesta."

"Then I will await your messages," said Ozymandias. "Till then . . ."

Without looking back, he walked past the fountain and into another part of the park. He did not know if Kartaphilos remained seated on the bench, or if he disappeared into the crowd.

CHAPTER 15

While under the service of the Zend Avestan government, Ozymandias learned that the country was not the villainous collection of technocrats that he had first imagined. Indeed, he discovered that the finest politics is the politics of expediency, that diplomacy is just another word for weakness, and that in the realm of international relations there are no blacks and no whites—only myriad shades of gray. He found that the Zend Avestans carried with them a characteristic that was not to be found in any other nation of the World: they truly believed in themselves. As a people, they were unified by a spirit so full of enthusiasm that it seemed to be an irresistible force. They went about their tasks with a great dedication fostered by the belief that they were doing the right thing.

Quick to learn, innovative in their own right, the scientists and manufacturers spent long hours in briefing sessions with Ozymandias. He dispensed facts, formulas, and techniques in massive quantities, tempering the information only when he knew that the current level of Avestan industry would be unable to practically apply it.

Within a year, Ozymandias had overseen the retooling of the nation's entire machine-shop industry. Once this was accomplished, there was no limit to the new developments made possible.

The armies were re-outfitted. New weapons, new vehicles, new training techniques.

Transportation systems were redesigned. Pipelines.
Highways. Bridges. Self-propelled methane vehicles.

Energy systems. Hydroelectric plants. Geothermal taps.
Solar collectors. Steam turbines. And finally the first new
nuclear reactor to generate power in more than three
millennia.

It was a geometric progression which, once begun, spread
beyond the control of any one man or group of men. The
original catalyst to all the furious activity—the breaking of
the Interdict by the Behistar barbarians—was dealt with in
an eyeflash. Within two weeks, after the Avestan Expeditionary Force had been mobilized, the Behistar Republic's
army and navy were totally destroyed. Fur-clad horsemen
wielding swords and crude flintlock rifles were no match
for the armored desert force designed by Ozymandias and
his staff.

For all intents, the country known as the Behistar Republic ceased to exist. Its small caste of aristocrats and
royal families was quickly imprisoned and the remainder of
its largely uneducated, primitive citizens were organized
into work and education camps. In less than a fortnight,
Zend Avesta had increased its store of natural resources
and the limits of its territory more than twofold. It took the
rest of the World little time to realize what was happening,
and despite the lack of sophisticated communications systems among the northern nations, a general assembly of
those nations' rulers and top advisers was called for.

Put as simply as possible, Zend Avesta planned to uplift
and civilize the rest of the World, and the rest of the World
refused to be civilized.

Ozymandias watched the development of international
politics escalate rapidly, and felt increasingly helpless to
have any influence on what would take place. The wealth
of historical data and the terrifyingly similar parallels to be

found in past conflicts were ignored by the government officials. Who could be concerned about the petty squabbles of long dead nations when what was needed was data on how more explosive force could be contained within a shell of limited size? Who felt it was necessary to study the lessons of history when everyone was trying to develop a dive bomber?

In the beginning, it was merely an economic conflict. Zend Avesta initially reeled under the international trade boycott which effectively removed it from access to raw materials, food supplies, and foreign currency. It was hoped by the leaders of the north that this action would bring Avesta to its senses and force an eventual reconciliation. What the northern leaders did not anticipate was the wealth of knowledge still to be tapped in Ozymandias.

Synthetic foods were created, raw materials were replaced with man-made substitutes, and the entire Avestan economy became driven by what was known as the "war effort." The current thinking by the Avestan officials was that the above measures would only be stopgap solutions. It would be far simpler, reasoned the government leaders; if the other gulf nations would not sell them what they needed, then they would be forced to simply take it.

Soon, the shipyards in Borat were alive with the sounds of steelworkers laying the beams for metal warships. A new navy was being constructed which would be the scourge of the entire Aridard Gulf. In the meantime, a mechanized army crossed the Samarkesh Burn, through what had once been Behistar, and into the headlands of the ancient battleground known as the Ironfields. From the north, the combined armies of G'Rdellia, Nespora, Shudrapur, Odo, the Scorpinnian Empire, even Pindar and Eyck, all converged in a massive column of horses, carts, cannon, and men.

The Armies of the Northern Alliance, as they came to call themselves, marched south to meet Zend Avesta in the headlands below the Straits of Nsin. It was a magnificent column of flesh and steel, of noise and flash. Their banners slipped proudly in the winds, their colors clashing as soon would be their swords.

It was a time of great excitement, and in such a time, as may be expected, some things are emphasized, and some things are forgotten. In the case of Ozymandias, the officials of the government became overly concerned with the war effort and the manifest destiny which they had taken on their shoulders, and had forgotten their promise to a father that he might occasionally see his son.

As time wore on, Ozymandias began to realize that his requests for a leave of absence, for even a few hours with his young boy, were being ignored. There was no time for such things, he was finally told. Personal affairs would have to be subordinated to the affairs of state. At least for the present. Did he not know that there was a *war* on?

Riding in the van of the Expeditionary Force, it would have been difficult for Ozymandias to be ignorant of such a fact. He had been commissioned into the army and given an obligatory staff position with the Council of Generals. While he felt it to be terribly ironic and fateful that his army marched close to the site of his birthplace, it was not his own suggestions that caused the event. He was fascinated by the cyclic movements of men and their history, however, and in his final days it was the one subject which held any interest for him at all.

Although Ozymandias had been a remarkably tough, inventive, and resilient human being, he found that he was growing weary of it all. In the short span of his life, there had been compressed into his experience enough to compensate for paucity of years. He had captured joys which few men ever knew; he had suffered agonies which few ever imagined. He had entered the world with an enthusiasm and a sincere desire to help humankind that almost constantly suffered tarnishment and corrosion from the influence and example of his fellow humans. The one thing which he never realized, never really accepted, was that the duality of human nature was immutable, that there was no changing the essential character of the human species. He did not realize that every man carried within his soul the seeds of growth and destruction in almost equal amounts, that everyone had the potential to improve or degrade himself, and everyone eventually did one or the other with lasting effects.

Ozymandias had never believed that humankind carried a specieswide death wish, a propensity for self-destruction that was almost a psychological *need*.

He had never believed it until now.

He knew that he would never see his son again. He knew that all his dreams would soon be shattered among the skeletal ruins of past dreams, among the deadly monuments of the Ironfields.

It is a terrible moment when a man reflects upon his works and can see only failure in his efforts. It is a time of despair and total desolation of the soul. The moment arrived for Ozymandias long after midnight as he lay awake in his field tent. All around him slept the rest of his staff, and beyond them the horde of soldiers in wait for their role in a new Final War.

He had been sleeping fitfully, but when he woke there was no memory of any alarming dream or nightmare. His brow glistened from a cool sweat and his hands were trembling. As he sat staring into the darkness, he struggled to compose a mental image of his young son's face, trying to imagine what the boy might look like as he entered his fifth year of life.

Five years.

The impact of the words, the concept, the passage, struck him.

He would not see Bysshe again, and he did not want to see Armageddon. He did not even want to return to the oblivion of sleep, for it was not oblivion enough. Each morning now only served to remind him of the perversion which had become his life. He had suffered through enough distortions of his ideals, enough degradations of his principles and destruction of his beliefs. For the first time, he recognized in himself that part of the human mind which is attracted to self-destruction. For the first time he saw sense in such reasoning, and saw a kind of salvation in that private path.

The lesson was at an end, he knew that now. The grand experiment had been completed, and it was a failure. The cycle had run its full course, and was seeking a new beginning. But before there can be a new beginning, there must be an end, and Ozymandias knew this. His final thoughts were of his son, and he hoped that in Bysshe's future things might be different.

And then he unstrapped his sidearm from its holster, placed the cool barrel against his temple, and fired a bullet through his brain.

EPILOGUE

News of the conflict had not reached him, but the gray-robed figure did not need to know the details. Whatever would be written or spoken of the battle would be familiar to him. It would be a tale told many times, and perhaps doomed to be repeated throughout the length of Time itself.

It mattered little to him at any rate. The more pressing concern was basic survival as he walked across the edge of the desert called the Samarkesh Burn. He traveled east, along a little known route which would eventually take him to the place of his birth, to a fortress called the Citadel, which would insulate him from the rest of the World—now a World gone mad.

The gray-robed figure had been resourceful, and he had been successful in his search for the child. In less than a year, he had been able to trace backward the path from the abbey to the convent on the shores of the Sunless Sea. Posing as a peripatetic monk, he gained entrance to the nunnery and kidnapped the child. He had been surprised that no great manhunt had been organized to track him down, and did not learn at first that the state had become concerned with higher priorities.

Time passed quickly for one who has seen a generation of centuries die. The child grew older, stronger, and wiser, but he had never known his father. The cyborg promised him that they would find his father, and after finally escaping the borders of Zend Avesta, they headed for the place where the armies of destiny always gathered.

They were a strange pair as they walked across the burning sands, a broad-shouldered man holding the small hand of a small bright-eyed boy. The gulf between them was as large as millennia, as small as the memory of a very special man, a man who called himself Ozymandias.

Someday, the boy would wish to know about his father, and it would fall upon Kartaphilos to tell him the tale. He did not know *what* he would say, or *how* he would say it.

But the path to the Citadel was long, and he would think of something . . .